F

P9-BHY-547

About the Book

Wonderful tales are told by the people who live in the colorful, exotic lands of the Middle East — tales in which marvelous good fortune comes to deserving folk and wicked folk are justly punished, tales of talking animals and kneeling trees, tales full of sounds, smells and tastes of their native lands.

The Kneeling Tree is a collection of seven stories from seven Mideastern lands. From Iran comes the story of clever Mirza and the Ghul; from Jordan, the tale of the Affable Lion whose friend, the Donkey, was stolen; from Turkey, the story of spindly Hamid who sought the help of the god Zanahari.

Dorothy Gladys Spicer has once more gathered together fresh, lively stories which she retells with imagination and verve. Her tales vividly bring to life the fascinating, mysterious lands of the Middle East, where anything can — and does — happen.

THE KNEELING TREE

The Kneeling Tree

AND OTHER FOLKTALES FROM THE MIDDLE EAST

by
DOROTHY GLADYS SPICER

Illustrated by BARBARA MORROW

Coward McCann   New York

Text copyright © 1971 by Dorothy Gladys Spicer
Illustrations copyright © 1971 by Barbara Morrow
All rights reserved. This book, or parts thereof, may not be reproduced in any form
without permission in writing from the publishers. Published simultaneously in Canada
by Longmans Canada Limited, Toronto.
Library of Congress Catalog Card Number: 78-106931
Printed in the United States of America

TO
MARIAN ROGER
Whom I met beside the Sea of Galilee

CONTENTS

THE KNEELING TREE

About These Tales

The area we call the Middle East is vast. From among the seventeen odd countries the territory includes, I have chosen tales from seven — Egypt, Iraq, Iran, Israel, Jordan, Syria and Turkey.

These mysterious lands have fascinated me since early childhood. I listened avidly to marvelous tales of wise talking birds and Middle Eastern potentates, patriarchs and prophets through whom God spoke. I cherished the treasures my parents gave me, such as tinkling camel bells and a silver charm fashioned into a hand — "the hand of the Prophet's daughter, Fatimah." Then there was a ring, handwrought in brass, set with white onyx and incised with an Arabic legend. Best of all were the olive wood beads, carved in Jerusalem, to help one pray;

the smooth dark-red "fidget" beads from who knows where, to help one think, and amber beads to wear and to touch. But most precious to me were the strings of flat round blue-green beads, with a staring eye in the center. *They* once hung between a Syrian donkey's ears, to protect the beast from harm and the Evil Eye!

As I grew up, I made many friends from the countries of my treasures. While I ate exotic foods, nibbled strange sweets, and sipped thick sweet coffee — "black as night and strong as love" — I heard the tales from their homelands. It was in those days that *The Kneeling Tree* really began.

When at last I visited the Middle East to gather material for this collection, many things I heard and saw were already familiar. The task of selecting so few stories from so great an area was awesome.

In the preparation of *The Kneeling Tree*, I read much, consulted aged folk wise in village lore, and talked with scholars, priests, and rabbis. Then I wrote in my own way the stories from their marvelous lands, where anything may happen — and does — as in my tales.

May you read with pleasure, visit these Middle Eastern countries one day, and discover their enchantment for yourself.

DOROTHY GLADYS SPICER

THE KNEELING TREE (Syria)

The orphan Salem lived in a Syrian town where he earned his bread by peddling *tarbooshes* — the tall red felt hats the Muslim men wear, with a tassel as a fez, or as turbans when wrapped around with cloth. All day the youth carried a heavy pack on his back, hawked his wares through the crooked lanes of the bazaar, and sold more tarbooshes in one hour than most peddlers in two. And since many Muslims gathered in the town to trade, gossip at coffeehouses, and worship at the mosque, there was a constant call for red hats.

Salem often succeeded in making sales where others failed, for besides having a nimble tongue, gentle manner and dazzling smile, he helped a customer make up his mind. When the youth placed a hat on the

15

head of a shriveled old man, stood back, and said, "Ah, yes, wear it this way, sir, for it suits your distinguished profile," or, "Suppose we try the tassel a little to the left," the old one somehow felt important and young. Usually he walked away wearing the tarboosh, and with a pleased smile on his lips.

It was small wonder the other peddlers envied Salem. Yet the youth deserved his success. Along with taking pains to please people, he offered them quality. "Shoddy goods attract shoddy buyers," he said. That was why he sold only the smoothest felts. His reds were the brightest, his dark-blue tassels the longest and made of real silk. And when it came to customers, Salem's were the most discriminating.

Although business was good, what with the high cost of merchandise and keep, Salem found it difficult to lay aside much for the donkey he longed to buy. For three years he scrimped and saved, yet the fund in the crock on the shelf grew slowly. "With a beast to help, I'd sell twice as many hats and be only half as tired at night," he'd sigh, as he trudged home so weary he could scarce drag one foot after the other. But the young man wasn't one to complain. No indeed! "What with donkeys dear and money scarce, I must be patient," he'd add with a grin. "By the time I'm too old and bent to carry a pack, I'll have enough saved to buy a beast — and need one more then than now!"

Thus several years passed, and then one day Salem's entire life changed.

That day, as usual, Salem had spent in the bazaar. It was dusk, his pack light and the crowd thinning, when a stranger spoke his name.

Salem turned in surprise, but before he could speak, the man lifted a hand. "The Christian priest of the hill village to the north, where your Great-Uncle Izan lived all his life, has sent me to find you and deliver a message," he said without wasting words. "Your great-uncle has died, and you are his heir. The Father begs you come at once and claim your inheritance."

"An — an *inheritance!*" Salem gaped. He just barely remembered hearing his mother speak of a beloved uncle in her home village. "But my great-uncle never saw me," the youth said. "And I never saw him. Why should he make me his heir?"

The messenger shrugged. "That is nothing to me. When shall I tell the Father to expect you?" he asked.

With an effort Salem pulled himself together. "How do I find the village? How far is it from here?" he asked, realizing all at once that he'd never been beyond the boundaries of the town.

"A two-day donkey ride by the road north," replied the stranger.

Salem thought quickly. If a beast could make the journey in two days, a young man with long legs could do it in three. "Please tell the Father I shall arrive three days hence," he told the messenger.

Early the next day, Salem set out, swinging over the miles with quick feet and a grateful heart. His thoughts flew back through the years to his dear mother. And thinking of her, he found himself fitting together all the pieces and bits she'd told him of "when I was a girl, lived in the hills and sat at the feet of my dear Uncle Izan."

"He was close to God," Salem's mother said of the old man. "He spoke only the truth, and the strength of his heart was rooted in faith. Each day he plodded from village to village, staff in hand and book under arm, to teach the little ones. They were his children." Then she added proudly, "He even taught me, *a girl,* to write my name, do sums and read verses from the Holy Book!"

Her Uncle Izan had taught the young girl other things as well — things she cherished and remembered her entire life. He'd told her stories of wonders and miracles. There were the Kneeling Trees, for example.

When his mother told him that story, Salem had shouted, *"But trees don't kneel!"* and added smugly, "Besides, dear Mother, no one believes in miracles!"

The youth had never forgotten the startled look on his mother's face when she said, sadly, "You are right, my son. No one in the towns believes in miracles — or in things not seen. But where *I* come from, in the hills, everyone does. Regardless of faith, everyone — Muslim as well as Christian — believes the miracle of the Kneeling Trees, though for different reasons. The Christians know the trees bow low each Epiphany Eve — January fifth — at the hour of twelve, in honor of the Lord Jesus. At that exact same hour, so said my Uncle Izan, the Star led the Three Kings to Bethlehem. They found the manger, laid their gifts of gold, frankincense and myrrh at the feet of Our Infant Jesus, and knelt in adoration.

"Ever since, in memory of that first Blessed Eve, hundreds of years ago," Salem's mother concluded, "the trees have knelt, also. They offer *their* precious gifts — fruits or berries or flowers — like the Magi of the East, incline their heads humbly and worship the King of Kings."

A miracle I'd have to see to believe, Salem had scoffed secretly. After his parents died, he learned he'd been right all along. The only *real* miracles came from sweat and hard work.

On the morning of the third day of his journey, Salem climbed a stony hill, turned a sharp bend, and gaped in astonishment. There before him lay his mother's village. "When I was a boy, she described it a hundred times," he whispered. There were the small square houses, with flat roofs and weathered walls, climbing the hill. There were the cypress and olive trees. And at the far end of the hamlet, gleaming white against an azure sky, was the cross of the church where she'd prayed as a girl.

As though in a dream, Salem ran through the village and knocked at the door of the small house near the church. An old priest wearing a carved olive wood cross on the bosom of his black robe welcomed Salem kindly. The Father drew him inside, and suddenly the young man had the odd feeling of having come home at last.

Before Salem was half done with the brimming bowlful of cracked wheat — *burghul* — the stack of fresh thin bread and the cooling clabbered milk — *laban* — which his host had set before him, he felt as though he'd known the old man all his life. Salem told the Father about his boyhood, his struggle to support himself after his parents died, and how, at last, he'd become his own man, as a tarboosh peddler. "I had only the best hats and the best customers," he said. "And if I'd had a donkey to help, I could have done better. I've been saving and scrimping for three years to buy one."

"Hmmm — m." The Father stroked his beard thoughtfully. "To peddle successfully takes a man with a special gift," he remarked. "Such a man might do well hereabouts. The Muslims in hamlets such as ours have as great a need for tarbooshes as the Muslims in towns, and less chance to buy new ones."

"Yes, a man might do well hereabouts — with a beast to help him over the hills," the youth agreed politely.

With the meal finished, the priest abruptly changed the subject. "Your great-uncle lost track of your dear mother after she married and your father took her away to the town," he explained. "The good man never heard from her again. When he was old, ill and his days numbered, a man who knew your father brought the sad news of your parents' untimely death and spoke of you, their only son. It was too late then to send for you, much to your great-uncle's sorrow. That was why he sent for me on his deathbed and charged me to find you and tell you his plan for your future."

"My mother spoke often of my great-uncle Izan's concern for others," murmured Salem, greatly moved.

"It was greater than his concern for himself," the priest nodded and continued. "Your great-uncle said, 'Salem is to have my house and my nest egg of a hundred pieces of silver — but on condition he promises to —' Here the old man's breath failed. I thought he had breathed his last. But his lids fluttered once more; he looked at me and said clearly, 'On condition he promises to care for Jasmine, *so long as she lives.*'

"Then he fell asleep forever, a smile on his lips," concluded the Father.

After a stunned instant, Salem moistened his lips and asked, "But who is Jasmine?"

The priest smiled. "Jasmine was the faithful friend of your great-uncle's old age. I shall take you to her after you see the property. Then you shall decide." The Father rose quickly, reached for his stick, and went to the door, saying, "Follow me," as he started up the hill.

The priest walked briskly, and Salem, his thoughts spinning, tagged behind. He'd just decided that Jasmine was probably some toothless crone who'd swept his great-uncle's house and prepared his food, when his guide stopped at a gate in a garden wall, turned with a smile, and lifted the latch. "Behold your own vine and fig tree, my son," he said grandly and led the youth into a small courtyard with a small house.

"Is this — is this *mine?*" gasped Salem, gazing around in delight. For in the center of the courtyard was a fig tree and under it a bench. Grapevines clambered over the garden wall, and beside the door of the house grew marjoram, thyme and other sweet herbs. "Did my great-uncle leave all this to *me?*"

"All this and more — if you agree to the condition, that is," the Father nodded and chuckled. Salem felt a stab of uneasiness, but before he had time to worry further about Jasmine, he was inside the small one-room house.

And now for the second time that day, Salem had the odd feeling that he'd come home. For everything he saw seemed familiar. Somehow he knew where everything was and felt he'd been here before. "It's all as my dear mother said," he murmured, glancing from the high grilled window to the clay jars against the wall, and the straw floor mats, woven around and around in purple, green and cerise. "And there's where she sat, at her Uncle Izan's feet and listened to his tales of kneeling trees and other miracles," he cried, pointing to a low, crudely fashioned child's stool in the corner.

"Tales I daresay you didn't believe as a boy," said the Father, fixing probing eyes on the young man's face.

"And still don't," Salem said, flushing in spite of himself. "*I must see, to believe,*" he declared.

"Ah, well, you may change — after you've lived in these hills awhile," replied the priest, stroking his beard. "Sometimes things we can't see are more real than those we can see," he said, and whisked Salem through the door. "We must pay our visit to Jasmine," the good man continued. He crossed the garden and stopped before a shed built cunningly into a corner of the wall. "Open the door," he directed.

All at once Salem's heart pounded. He lifted the latch with trembling fingers, pushed open the door, and his eyes met the innocent gaze of a small white donkey with long velvet ears. She uttered a friendly bray, and Salem ran forward with arms outstretched.

How long he embraced the little beast, rubbed her long ears, and patted her flanks, while she, in turn, nuzzled his neck, Salem didn't know. But when the Father cleared his throat and said, "Well?" and then asked dryly, "Have you decided, my son, to accept your great-uncle's condition?" Salem looked up with a sheepish grin.

"*Have* I?" he exclaimed, his eyes like stars. "I promise to care for Jasmine so long as she lives, and wish it might be for a hundred years!"

Thus Salem came to be the happiest young man in Syria, and Jasmine the most beloved beast. For now, what with his nest egg to invest in a big store of merchandise, the kind Father's help and Jasmine, he was soon peddling tarbooshes from village to village.

Each morning Salem fastened willow panniers on the small donkey's back, filled them with red hats and hung blue beads around her neck to keep her from harm. "Thank you, thank you, dear Great-uncle, for such kindness to a youth you never saw," he'd say in gratitude as they left the courtyard and jogged up the hill.

From the first, the pair prospered. For never had the Muslims of the hamlets seen such fine red hats. They all liked Salem, and after business was completed, they ordered their wives to prepare coffee and sweets, and their sons to tend Jasmine, while they looked after "our honored guest."

As summer turned to autumn, Salem happily told the priest, "I have paid for my investment."

"And soon will double it," replied the Father proudly. "You have an old head on young shoulders, my son."

"And Jasmine to help me," Salem reminded him, stroking her white velvet ears.

Christmas passed, and so did the New Year. Epiphany Eve — the day before Epiphany — dawned clear and cold. "Business should be good in the villages today, what with the chief festivities of *Muharram* ahead — the Muslim New Year — the visits and calls and need for finery," Salem told Jasmine and filled her panniers, as usual, with red hats.

But Salem was mistaken. The Muslim men weren't thinking of finery. A hush of expectancy pervaded the hamlets, and many were meditating, or reading the *Koran*.

After Jasmine had jogged up hill and down, stopped at five villages, and still they'd not sold a single tarboosh, her master was sorely troubled. At last he asked his old friend, Abu Ganin, "What is the matter? Today no one buys."

"And no one will," replied the old man with a smile and advised the youth to go home. "Tonight is *Lailat-al-Qadr* — The Night of Destiny. No Son of the Prophet will buy today."

"But *why?*" the young man persisted, more puzzled than before. "What *is* the Night of Destiny?"

"It's easy to see you've not heard about our tradition, my son," replied Abu Ganin kindly. "Centuries ago on this night, Allah sent his angel to the Prophet Mahomet, to deliver the sacred writings of the Koran. Ever since, the trees have bowed to earth in honor of Allah's revelation to man."

"The Kneeling Trees, eh?" Salem mused, thanked the old man, and turned Jasmine toward the long steep slope that led from the village. And now the youth once more recalled his mother's words, "In the hills everyone — Christian and Muslim — believes that the trees kneel, though for different reasons."

"How foolish can everyone be?" Salem asked Jasmine, when they reached the bottom of the slippery hill and he led her into the courtyard of the Christian Rashid's hospitable coffeehouse.

The little beast flopped her ears forward wisely as Salem tethered her to a low branch of a cypress tree, ordered water and food, and threw his cloak over her back. "Stuff your stomach, little one, while I drink coffee. And when we're both rested, we'll go home to our beds." And so saying, Salem entered the coffeehouse.

"Welcome, my friend," cried Rashid, with a pleased smile. He bade his wife, Bassiemie, to fetch coffee and pastries, led his guest to a pan of glowing coals in the corner, and asked, "How was business today?"

"Never worse," grumbled Salem. "For the first time Jasmine is taking home as many red hats as she took out this morning. Everywhere the men folk are too busy reading the Koran and babbling of the miracle of the Kneeling Trees to so much as look at a tarboosh!"

"Ah, yes, on this Blessed Eve, 'Christians and Muslims are brothers,' so your Great-uncle Izan used to tell us," Rashid said, stroking his beard. "Whether we believe the trees kneel in honor of Jesus, or of the Koran, regardless of our faith all of us believe the miracle."

"Hmmm-m," mocked Salem, accepting a third cup of thick sweet black coffee and a third nut-and-honey pastry. "A miracle *I'd* have to see to believe!"

How many cakes he ate or cups of coffee he drank before Jasmine's loud frightened brays shattered the air, Salem didn't know. But when he flew to the courtyard with Rashid and Bassiemie at his heels, glanced around quickly, and didn't see Jasmine, he thought at first a thief was dragging her away. Still, the distressed "hee-haws" were close and seemed to come from somewhere overhead. And when the moon darted from behind a cloud and flooded the courtyard with bright eerie light, the young man was even more mystified. For now he saw the rope dangling limply from the tree branch, red tarbooshes littering the ground, and his cloak lying beside them in a lump. "Jasmine, Jasmine, where *are* you?" he cried, seized by sickening fear.

But the answering "Hee-haw, *Hee-haw,* HEE-HAW" left no doubt about where Jasmine was! Salem looked up. And when, in the bright moonlight, he saw Jasmine — her small body shining white against the dark dense upper branches of the tree — he knew what had happened. "It's the miracle!" he shouted, and Bassiemie and Rashid sank to their knees in awe. "The tree *did* kneel, and when it snapped back, it swept up Jasmine and carried her to the topmost branches."

"I'll fetch a ladder and rope to rescue her," cried the practical Rashid, now on his feet and running to the stable.

But before he returned, a second miracle took place, or so Salem later told the Father in describing the events of that Epiphany Eve.

For now, as Jasmine heard her master speak comforting words, she lost her fear, her wild brays ceased, and she slid lower and lower, from one branch to another. The great cypress tree seemed to bow graciously, the thick full branches sustained her, and she suffered no harm. "Be brave, little one, soon you'll be safe," Salem cried and held out his arms.

And soon Jasmine was. When she felt her master's arms about her, she nestled close, the quivering of her small body ceased, and soon she was able to stand alone.

"God has blessed us all this night," whispered Bassiemie, her face shining.

"And chosen a humble beast to teach her witless master that miracles do happen," Salem said, clasping Jasmine.

From that Epiphany Eve, Salem never scoffed again at God's wonders. As for Jasmine, she lived happily and long. In the Syrian hills, to this day folk call the donkey the Blessed Beast.

So blessed indeed is the small donkey to the boys and girls in many parts of Syria that they say she never died, like other creatures. "On Epiphany Eve she enters the house with blessings and gifts," they declare. Only at midnight can anyone see her. And though the children fling doors wide to receive her, prop their lids open, and try to keep awake, at that hour, alas, little ones are fast asleep.

MIRZA AND THE GHUL   (Iran)

Long ago in Persia — which is now called Iran — everyone, from His Glorious Majesty, the Shah, to the meanest slave, lived in fear of the *Ghul* — everyone, that is, save brash young Mirza. From earliest boyhood, Mirza never feared anything!

Ghuls were huge evil demons with burning eyes and itchy fingers. They dwelt in caves on the broad steppes east of Isfahan. And whenever anything unpleasant happened in villages or towns — a foul murder, the disappearance of a widow's cow or greasy *dinars* from a beggar's hoard — people blamed the Ghul. "He was here in the night," they said, blanching.

Yet no matter how much the old feared the Ghul, boys and girls

29

feared him more. "He was the bogey their parents frightened them with," say the folk of modern Iran, eyes twinkling. "That's why children were better-mannered then than now."

All a mother had to do, it seems, was threaten, "If you don't stop teasing your brother, the Ghul will get you! He'll lug you to his cave like a sack of meal, eat your flesh, and gnaw your bones," and the terrified little one behaved like an angel in paradise!

But the lad Mirza was different. At the mention of Ghuls, *he* scoffed and defied his elders. There was the day his grandfather, who reared him after his parents died, caught him stealing sweets. When the old man rolled his eyes, clacked his tongue, and remarked, "Ahhh—h, the Ghul will carry you off in the night," the child rudely stamped his foot.

"Ho, ho, who's afraid of a Ghul?" jeered Mirza. *"Ghuls aren't real!* Only silly old men believe they are."

"Only silly small boys believe they're *not!*" retorted his grandfather and turned his back.

It wasn't until Mirza had grown from a stubborn boy into a tall handsome youth, with merry eyes, heart of gold and brash, swaggering ways, that he had cause to remember these words. That was some time after he'd gone to Isfahan to seek his fortune. "I'll apprentice myself to a cobbler, learn the craft of mending shoes, and then send for you, dear Grandfather," Mirza said eagerly, on taking fond leave of the old man.

From the first, things worked out well for the youth. He apprenticed himself to old Abdul Ali, liked him and the craft, and took pains to learn it. From dawn to dark, Mirza sat cross-legged on the floor of the small dim shop and mended with a cunning that amazed his master. "Whatever task I set him, whether to repair the turned-up toe of a boot or the turned-down heel of an old sloppy slipper, he does it with skill," he boasted to his friend, the baker. "I can scarcely tell where my apprentice's patches end or where they begin. I predict one day he'll become a master cobbler, skilled as I, Abdul Ali myself," he declared.

And so thought Mirza. As time passed, his skill increased, and he did more mending in a day than a dozen pairs of hands could usually manage in a week. *When I'm my own man, I'll send for dear Grandfather, and he'll never have to plow and plant for the rich folk again,* he thought happily as he pounded pegs, stitched tops to soles, and turned old shoes into new.

Then one day Mirza's plans changed abruptly. That was the day the baker rushed through the door with his startling news. *"Ah wahi, ah wahi,* what are we coming to?" he wailed, waving his arms. "Last night a thief broke into the Shah's treasury, stole his priceless pearl, and escaped. Folks say it's a bad omen. The Shah gave the pearl to his beloved dead wife — the Princess Simha's mother — when he married her. The gem was to be his daughter's the day she wed. But now, alas, the pearl is gone, and no one is like to ever see it," he ended sadly. "In spite of the rich reward, no one will dare risk his life in the search because of — because of— "

"Because of *what?*" prompted Abdul Ali, when the baker seemed ready to collapse. And although Mirza kept on pounding, he pricked up his ears at mention of the reward.

"Because of the mark the palace guard found this morning on the garden wall — the mark of a Ghul's great hand!" the baker whispered, his face ashen.

Before his master had time to reply, Mirza's scornful laugh peeled through the small shop. "Ha, ha, ha, the mark of a Ghul's hand, indeed!" he mocked. "As if Ghuls were real! A careless guard made the mark himself and trumped up a tale to save his own neck!"

The baker stared coldly. "His Majesty, the Shah, doesn't think so, young man," he said, after a shocked pause. "If he did, he'd hardly offer seven bags of gold to the brave man who brings back the pearl — and twice as much, for proof the Ghul took it."

For an instant Mirza's head reeled. "Seven bags of gold, eh?" he muttered and then and there made up his mind to search for the pearl. *What with everyone else afraid of both the demons and the caves, I might just find it,* he thought gleefully. For now he recalled other tales he had heard. There were always caves in those stories — caves where long ago cutthroats stored silks and jewels after attacking caravans. "That's the first place a clever thief would choose to store a priceless pearl today — till the hubbub died down," the youth decided.

The next day Mirza rose before dawn, stuffed enough flat bread and curd cheese for a day's journey into the woven bag at his belt, and crept out the door. "With Allah's help and a bit of luck, I'll be back with the pearl before Abdul Ali misses me," he said, chuckling. "And when I get the gold and give him a nest egg for his old age, he'll forgive me." And there was dear Grandfather. *He'd* live like a prince, and he, Mirza, would have his own shop.

As Mirza sped through dim alleys and narrow, twisty lanes, his thoughts flew faster than his feet. He reached the east gate just at sunrise. When the golden rays bathed the blue-green mosaics in splendor, he murmured, " 'Tis a good omen." Then he passed under the arch and strode toward the steppes.

But they were farther than Mirza supposed. After he'd journeyed one day — and then two — and still seemed no closer to the steppes than when he had left Isfahan — he grew uneasy. When he rose from a bed of stones at dawn on the third day, he was so stiff he could hardly move. After he'd eaten his last crumb of bread, he eyed the cheese hungrily. But, "I'll save *that* till I find the first cave," he said stoutly.

Night was falling when Mirza limped into a wide stony plain, so weary he could hardly drag one foot after the other. There was something ominous about the desolate place. But when he spied the dark, yawning mouth of a cave nearby, he whooped, propped himself against a rock for support, and reached into his bag for the cheese.

Mirza's fingers had scarcely closed around the moist lump when an angry bellow from somewhere behind him sent shivers up his spine. For now a rough voice bawled, "Hey, you miserable pip-squeak from goodness knows where, how dare you come to *my* plain, loll against *my* rock, and stare at *my* cave?"

Mirza spun around quickly. When he saw the huge, ugly fellow — tall as a palm tree, with the girth of seven men — lumbering toward him, upraised club in hand, his heart plummeted to the soles of his feet. He didn't need to be told that he was face-to-face with a Ghul. All at once, he knew that Ghuls *were* real and he'd best think quickly if he wanted to live. It was clutching at the cheese inside his bag that gave him a splendid idea.

"I dare come here because I choose to — that's why," Mirza managed to say in a steady voice. "And though you *fancy* you're stronger, because you're a big bully, you're weak as a baby compared to me."

"Why, you — you skinny, impertinent ninny," bawled the Ghul. Purple with rage, he advanced a step. "Before I kill you, I'll teach you to sneer at a Ghul. I'll show you how strong I am." And so saying, he seized a stone as big as Mirza's head, crushed it to powder and blew it into the youth's face. "Ha! What do you think of *that?*"

"I think you're puny — for such a big Ghul," retorted Mirza with a contemptuous laugh. "It's easy enough to *crush* a stone. Any fool can do that. But to squeeze water from it takes *strength!*" He bent and selected a stone, and then his fingers flew so quickly 'twixt stone in hand and cheese in bag that the demon couldn't see *what* he was doing.

Mirza held out his hand and squeezed what the stupid Ghul supposed was the stone. And when moisture oozed slowly through his fingers, dripped to the ground and puddled at the youth's feet, fear crept into the demon eyes, and his jaw dropped. "For one so spindly, you're stronger than I thought," he admitted.

"Oh, that's nothing — compared to what I *can* do," Mirza said modestly, pleased at the success of his ruse.

The demon tried to conceal his fright by a show of friendliness. Yet at the same time his demon-mind was bent on destroying Mirza. Given time, the Ghul was certain he'd think of something. "Come," he invited Mirza with a toothy smile. "Share some rice with me in my cave, and in the morning we'll go on a hunting trip."

Mirza didn't fancy the notion. Still, he'd tricked the fellow once and could do so again, with luck. *If I'm to get the pearl and win the gold, I must search the cave*, he thought to himself. For now he was convinced the Ghul was the thief.

Aloud, Mirza said with feigned pleasure, "That's kind of you, Ghul. I can do with hot food and a spot of sleep."

"Come along then." The demon smirked, shouldered his club, and led the way through the fast-falling dusk.

The cave was foul and dark. Bones littered the stone floor, skins and sacks lay in heaps near the walls and on the wide hearth, dying embers cast eerie shadows. "I'll stir up the fire; you go to the spring and fetch water for the pot," the Ghul said and pointed to a water skin in the corner.

When Mirza saw the size of the skin, made of three ox hides sewn together, he had a bad moment. To drag it across the floor empty would tax his strength, let alone lift it filled with water! "Since it's dark, I might lose my way to the spring," he said. "We're both hungry, so let's not waste the time." Mirza spoke so boldly that the demon, remembering the stone, gaped, then tossed the skin over his shoulder, and stomped sullenly to the door. "This way, we'll get the water boiling sooner and eat quicker," the youth added, poking at the embers.

As the Ghul tramped away, the ground shook and Mirza's fingers flew. He laid kindling, fanned the embers into flame, and dragged heavy logs from a pile beside the huge fireplace. Only after the wood crackled and blazed and ruddy sparks chased up the chimney did he spring to his feet and start to search for the gem.

Mirza ran his fingers beneath the bones and sacks, explored crevices, and reached into crannies and holes. When at last, in a niche at the far end of the cave, he felt something fuzzy and soft as a kitten's ear, he shouted, "I've found it," and drew forth the object.

When Mirza discovered he was clutching a small, white, plush pouch embroidered in gold with the Shah's arms, with a great lustrous pearl inside — a pearl that gleamed like a full moon in a winter sky — his jaw dropped, and he teetered back on his heels.

The next instant, the ground quaked. Mirza had barely time to stuff the pouch inside his tunic, leap back to the hearth, and pick up the poker before the Ghul appeared at the door. "The fire's ready!" the youth called in what he hoped was a casual voice. "You can fill the pot and cook the rice."

But the trip to the spring hadn't improved the hungry demon's temper. He hung a huge blackened pot over the fire, slopped in water, and poured in half a sackful of rice. Only when a mountain of white fluffy grains overflowed the kettle did the Ghul grunt, "Supper's ready."

The demon swung the pot from the fire to the floor, and slapped wooden bowls down on either side of the kettle. "Sit down and help yourself," he told Mirza, who was perched on the half-empty sack. He watched in disgust as his host scooped up rice with his great hairy hands. Then the youth filled his own bowl.

It wasn't till the Ghul had helped himself seven times — and Mirza was still on his first bowlful — that his host smacked his lips, wiped his mouth on a hairy hand, and observed, "Hmmm—mm, you're skinny, of course. And you don't eat much for one so strong."

"Aha, but that's why I am strong," boasted Mirza, flexing an arm. "What I lack in bulk, I make up for in muscle. Now if *you* didn't stuff yourself, Ghul, weren't so flabby and fat, you'd be —"

"I'd be *what?*" roared the demon, eyes flashing.

"You'd be stronger, have more muscle and be able to do *simple* things — such as squeezing water from stones," Mirza finished complacently.

The huge fellow sprang to his feet, kicked the pot with the toe of a goatskin sandal, and bellowed, "You'll keep a civil tongue in your head, young man, when addressing a Ghul." But when Mirza laughed softly and doubled a fist, the demon thought better of picking a quarrel. "I'm tired and need my rest," he said. "Besides, we rise early."

The Ghul tossed a sheepskin to Mirza. "Nights are cold, and you'd best sleep near the hearth," his host said. And when he added, slyly,

"I'll lie before the door with my club and keep off prowling wolves," the youth knew he was up to no good.

Cold shivers raced up Mirza's spine — until his glance fell on the half-empty rice sack. Then he hugged himself to keep from laughing. "Good night, Ghul," he said, stretching out before the fire and making a great to-do of tucking the sheepskin around him. "I'm a sound sleeper. Be sure to call me tomorrow."

"I shall, never fear," the Ghul grunted with a chilling laugh.

When the demon's snores finally rattled like thunder through the cave, Mirza rose and crept toward the rice sack. By pulling and tugging an inch at a time, he somehow managed to drag the sack to the spot he'd just been occupying. *Lucky for me the thing's only half full,* he thought, pausing to wipe sweat from his brow. Then he deftly tucked the sheepskin around the sack and crouched behind the kettle to wait.

How long he waited, the youth didn't know. But it must have been past midnight when the snores turned to snorts and then stopped abruptly. Presently, by the flickering firelight, Mirza saw the Ghul ease himself to one elbow, cock his ear, and then reach a stealthy hand toward his club. The next instant he crept across the floor and bent over the bundle of sheepskin.

Then suddenly, WHAM, *WHAM,* down came the cudgel on the sheepskin. "Ho, ho, my spindly friend," shouted the Ghul. "That will teach you to tangle with a Ghul!" With a final W-H-A-M, he lumbered back to his place and lay down to sleep.

When loud snores rattled once more through the cave, Mirza crept back under the sheepskin. And now he set up a commotion of slapping, mutterings, and cries of annoyance — first this side, then that — which roused the Ghul. "W-what's the m-matter?" the demon jabbered, sitting up in a daze and staring in horror at Mirza. "What's h-happened?"

"Oh, nothing really — and I'm sorry I woke you, Ghul," grunted Mirza, slapping at an imaginary insect. "Do you have gnats or mosquitoes . . . or maybe spiders . . . in your cave? When I was asleep just now, something nipped my shoulder several times."

The Ghul's eyes bulged. "You measly little runt," he howled, scrambled to his feet, and fled from the cave, shrieking, "I can't even kill you — but you might k-kill m-me!"

As the demon's yells died away in the distance, Mirza rolled on the ground in mirth. "If only you knew, Ghul," he said when he was able to speak. "I haven't even strength to twist your little finger! But I have the pearl, and I shall get the reward," he added and patted the bag inside his tunic.

But Mirza didn't get to Isfahan so soon as he'd planned. For just then, a yell shattered the air and the cave shook with a terrific crash — as if a mighty tree were toppling to earth. Moans followed — then deathly silence. Mirza rushed out to the wide stony plain. Gray dawn streaked the sky when at last he found the Ghul. He'd fallen on the rocks with such force that he had smashed his head in. The youth shuddered and muttered, "Good riddance!"

Not until he saw the awful sight did he remember the Shah's offer — *twice*-seven bags of gold to any one who brought him proof that the

Ghul had stolen his gem. "And here it is!" cried Mirza, eyes sparkling. He stooped and tugged the goatskin sandals — thrice the size of an ordinary big man's — from the dead giant's feet. He tied the long leather thongs together and thereupon set off joyfully for Isfahan.

Mirza's heart felt light as a feather, what with carrying the pearl next to his bosom and dragging at his heels the huge heavy shoes, making sounds like a horse's hooves.

Three days and two nights later, Mirza arrived at the gate of the royal palace, his garments torn and covered with dust. He knocked boldly and told the guard he had urgent business with His Majesty, the Shah. The guard laughed. "His Majesty doesn't see beggars," he said and raised a threatening arm.

"The Shah will see me," said Mirza, drawing himself up proudly. "I am no beggar, and you will take me to him if you are wise." He reached inside his shirtfront, drew forth the small bag embroidered with the imperial arms, and dangled it before the gaping guard. The fellow blanched, mumbled incoherently, and forthwith led Mirza to the audience chamber.

But when the Shah, seated on his throne in jeweled turban and brocade robes and surrounded by three-and-twenty bearded viziers, glanced up and saw the disheveled youth, his eyes blazed in anger. "Who are you?" he thundered. "How dare you come to your Shah in tattered garments, with dirt on your face and those — those —" Words failing, he pointed a jeweled finger at the huge goatskin sandals.

Mirza bowed low before his sovereign, touched his brow thrice to the blue-green tiles at his feet, and spoke without fear. "I am the cobbler's apprentice, Mirza," said he. "For my appearance I crave your Majesty's indulgence. But I have journeyed in haste from the eastern steppes, to restore your pearl and to show Your Royal Highness that the Ghul did indeed rob you. In proof, I bring the sandals I took from his feet." Then, before the astonished Shah could reply, he drew from his tunic the white plush bag and placed it upon the royal palm.

In the silence that followed this revelation, the viziers leaned forward, pulling at their beards. The Shah stepped from his throne, embraced Mirza, and said kindly, "Our words were hasty, our gratitude is great, and so shall be your reward." Then he commanded him to relate his adventure from beginning to end.

When Mirza finished his story, the Shah laughed till tears coursed down his cheeks. "Any youth brave enough to go alone to the steppes, recover my pearl, and outwit a Ghul is brave enough to be my son," he declared.

Then, to the youth's consternation, the Shah commanded slaves to fetch his daughter, the beautiful Princess Simha. And now Mirza, remembering he'd been reared to speak the truth, hung his head in shame. "I — I am unworthy to receive such an honor," he confessed, moistening his lips. "I wasn't brave, but *brash!* I never believed the Ghul was real! If I had, I'd not have had courage to seek the pearl," he ended wretchedly.

"But you had courage to tell your Shah the truth, my son," said the ruler, an arm around the youth's shoulders. "And that is far more important."

Now the slaves brought the Princess to her father's presence. He lifted the shimmering veil from her face and placed her small hand between Mirza's toil-hardened palms.

When Mirza dared lift his eyes and found himself gazing into those of the beautiful maiden, sudden happiness surged over him. For seeing the goodness and radiance in her face, he knew he had met the only girl he could ever love.

And the Princess, on her part, was for the first time head-over-heels in love. No prince in the land had such merry eyes, such an honest smile, or was half as handsome as this young man in tattered clothes, with a smudge on his nose!

Great was the joy of all — from the proudest prince to the meanest slave — when they learned their lovely Princess was to wed the cobbler's apprentice, Mirza, "the only man on earth brave enough to seek the pearl and frighten the Ghul to his death," they said.

On her wedding day, no bride was as beautiful as Princess Simha. When her father saw her — in her floating white robe embroidered with threads of silver, on her brow a silver circlet set with the great glowing pearl, and on her lips a radiant smile — he declared, "She is more lovely than her mother on *her* wedding day!"

As for young Mirza, no prince was as splendid — in his silken robes, jeweled turban, and around his slim waist a belt studded with three-score-seven sparkling diamonds. Of him, the monarch predicted, "When he ascends the throne and rules in my stead, he will be a clever Shah."

And the Shah was right, as later events proved. For when he died and

Mirza ascended the throne, he was both clever and just. He ruled for many years, his beloved Simha at his side, and the land prospered. As long as he lived, Mirza cared for the poor and fought the cause of the weak. To this day, the storytellers of Persia speak with pride of "Shah Mirza the Great."

3

THE SEVEN-YEAR BLESSING   (Israel)

God's messenger on earth, the Prophet Elijah, unlike other men, did not taste death. The *Bible* tells us that God transported him. When Elijah's hour came, God sent a fiery chariot through the skies to the banks of the River Jordan, to bear him away in glory.

Where the Bible story ends, legend begins. "From that day, God sent Elijah as His messenger to earth many times, to test the hearts of men, report their doings, and recommend punishment or reward," say the old folk of Israel. "The Prophet comes in many guises — as a beggar with dragging step, a weary stranger, a rich man or a prince. And some-times — as at the Seder Feast — Elijah is invisible. He glides like a ghost through the open door, takes his place in the empty seat at the table, and observes everything the merrymakers do or think."

Then the old ones go on to tell of the poor man Nathan, his wife, Leah, and their five sons, who lived so long ago that no one recalls when it was or the name of their village. "God sent the Prophet to test them," the storytellers say, as they begin their tale:

One Sabbath Eve God summoned the Prophet and commanded, "Visit earth and seek out the poor man, Nathan. He is in the market-place, has no work and no food for his family. Offer him seven years of prosperity and a choice of when he wishes to take them. Then return with word of his decision."

In accordance with God's instructions, Elijah disguised himself as a rich man, with a long white beard, silken robes and a cloak lined with fur. He descended to earth and went to Nathan's village. No sooner had he entered the market square than the Prophet singled out the poor man. He stood unnoticed among the happy jostling throng of shoppers, who were hurrying home with baskets laden with feast-day foods, candles and children's sweets. Nathan alone had nothing for the Sabbath, not even a farthing for bread or meal. He peered around anxiously. But when he approached first one shopper, then another, and offered his services, no one needed help with their bundles. "It's nothing but food tonight," everyone said and hurried on.

Food, Nathan reflected dejectedly. No matter how bulky it might look, *that* wasn't heavy — at least not in *his* experience! He sighed, shivered in the cool air, and drew his cloak closer — the cloak Leah had darned so often that no one could tell anymore what the color had been or whether the fabric were cotton or wool.

As God's messenger approached, he saw the poor man's lips move and heard the desperate words "Dear God, please send me work, help me, and let me earn a few coins, at least. I — I don't want to ask for charity, but all day no one has hired me and —"

"I'll help you," said the disguised Prophet's voice from somewhere behind Nathan. "All you have to do is listen — and make a decision."

Nathan spun around quickly. And when he saw the richly dressed old man, he thought God had heard his prayer and sent a customer. "How — how may I serve the gentleman?" he asked, and glanced about for a package, box or even papers to carry. Seeing nothing, his face fell. He gulped back his disappointment and blurted, "Is there an errand to run, a message to carry, or perhaps some special service to perform?"

The stranger smiled, lifted a jeweled finger, and said, "Listen, Nathan. In passing, I heard what you said. I'll give you and your family seven years of prosperity — with all the gold you want. If —"

Nathan blanched, moistened his lips, and whispered fearfully, "If *what*?" His head reeled, his hands were clammy, and his knees knocked together in terror, because he remembered what his grandfather had said when he, Nathan, was a young boy, "Beware of rich strangers, my son.

The Devil, a wolf in sheep's clothing, may come to tempt you with gold and a life of ease — in return for your soul. Trust only in God and the sweat of your brow."

"W-who are you?" Nathan faltered. "Whence do you come, and how do you know my name, unless —"

"No, Nathan, though I come from far, I am neither Devil nor sorcerer," replied the stranger, reading his companion's thoughts. "*Who* I am does not matter — for now. I know many things and have vast riches. You have nothing to fear. My offer, as I told you, is for seven good years. But you must choose whether to take them now, while you are young and strong, or later, when you are old and feeble and too weak to work."

"And after the good years?" Nathan asked, interested in spite of himself.

"All will be the same as now," said the stranger. "After all the gold you've had to spend on meat and drink, a house that's a palace, and more silks and jewels for Leah than a dozen queens could wear, you'll be poor again. You'll be standing here, as today, without work, no money in your purse, and nothing for your family to eat."

By this time Nathan, more frightened than before, tried to make excuses and edge away. "Thank you, kind sir, but we have all we need," he mumbled. "Besides, I'd have to consult my wife before I could make such a choice. She is wise and makes all decisions in our family."

"Then hasten, consult with your wife, and I shall await her decision," said the mysterious stranger with so much authority Nathan dared not disobey. "The counsel of a wise woman is worth more than rubies."

All the way home, Nathan's mind whirled with doubts about the old man. What would folk who'd always been poor do with riches? And what would Leah say when she heard of his remarkable offer?

When at last Nathan reached the door of their tumbledown hut, in the midst of a stony field beyond the village, he listened in dismay. From within came the sound of hopeless weeping. When he rushed inside the house, there was Leah huddled on a stool, apron over her face, sobbing as though her heart would break "It's — it's our sons," she wailed, when she could speak. "Today the Rabbi had to send them home from school, b-because —"

"Because we couldn't even pay the small fee he asks to teach them," Nathan finished. "And the Rabbi is right. He has long been generous. Like us, he is poor, has many mouths to feed, and earns little. But now, dear wife, dry your tears, for I have news that can change everything," he went on and told Leah about the mysterious stranger, his offer of gold and the decision they must make. "The choice of when to take the good years rests with you," he ended, his voice troubled. "For my part, despite his words, I can't tell whether the stranger comes from God, is a magician, a madman — or even a Devil."

But there was no doubt in Leah's mind. "God sent the stranger to help our sons," she said, clasping her thin hands, and added without hesitation, "We must accept the offer of prosperity now, while they are young, their heads filled with dreams, and their future ahead."

"But what of *ours?*" questioned Nathan. "What of the time when we are feeble and old, and I am unable to run errands and carry burdens?"

"God will take care of us then, as in the past," Leah cried, her face shining. "Our sons' future is *now*. Without learning they will be plodding peasants like us. With the stranger's gold to nourish their minds and feed their bodies, they can study in Jerusalem with great teachers, go into the world, and repay their debt. They will look after us when we cannot work. The gold and the learning both come from God," she concluded.

And now Nathan, convinced of the wisdom of Leah's words, cried joyfully, "As always, you are right, dear one. I shall return to the stranger and tell him your decision."

Dusk was falling when Nathan reached the square. The hurrying shoppers had gone, and the old man paced impatiently. "Well?" he asked testily. "What does Leah say?"

"Please, good Father, she says we'd like the good years now — for the sake of our sons," said Nathan, bowing low before the old man.

The stranger smiled, stroked his beard, and when he replied his voice was kind. "Your wife is wise, as you say, Nathan. Go home, receive your blessing, and we shall meet — seven years hence."

When the peasant lifted his eyes to thank the old man, he was nowhere in sight. The place where he had stood glowed with light, and a peace such as he'd never known filled Nathan's heart. "God answered my prayer," he murmured in awe. "God sent the stranger to help us."

Nathan raced home, through the village and across the field. As he neared the hovel, the door burst open, and out spilled his five sons, followed by their mother. "Hurry, dear Father, hurry," piped the youngest, a wispy lad of seven. "There it was, in the corner, when we returned from Mother's errand — the chest with — with —"

"Iron-bound corners, a huge lock, and a long key," cried the eldest son, swinging his brother onto his shoulders.

"Waiting for you, dear husband, to return," Leah took up the story, smiling. She grasped Nathan's hand and led him to the chest.

Thereupon, surrounded by his sons, Nathan turned the key in the lock and threw back the lid of the coffer. And when a stream of glittering golden shekels poured like water to the floor, he gaped in astonishment, the youths "oh-ed" and "ah-ed," and Leah clasped her hands.

After seconds or minutes — Nathan didn't know which — he reached out a finger and touched one round, shining coin. "I — I have never seen a piece of gold before — much less a chestful," he told his sons. Then he went on to tell of the stranger who had given the treasure and promised them seven years of plenty. "Your mother and I accepted both the gold and the years for you," he said, scanning the eager faces. "The gold is yours to use — as much as you need — to give you learning, help you grow in grace and enter the world, each in his chosen work."

"Think well, my sons," added Leah. "You have but to choose what you want to be. The gold will provide the means."

In the silence that followed their parents' words, each youth searched his heart. Then each, from the eldest to the youngest, expressed the inmost cherished hope that he had never thought to realize. "I shall study medicine, learn about the ills of men and how to heal them," their firstborn said joyfully.

"And I shall learn to defend the poor and the oppressed and see justice done," said the next son.

The third son's face flushed with pleasure. "I'll be a teacher," he announced. "I'll teach boys like us, too poor to pay for schooling."

"Now I can study the stars!" cried the fourth son. "I'll trace their course in the heavens through the eye of a great telescope, learn of seasons, tides, and when men should plant seed in the earth."

"And you, my son?" Nathan asked, drawing his youngest son toward him.

"Please, dear Father, I wish to be a Rabbi," the small boy said shyly, "study the Holy Torah and learn the great mysteries."

"And so you shall," his father cried and gathered the boy in his arms. "You all have chosen wisely," he told them proudly. "Use the gold well, fill your minds with God's wisdom, and when the seven years of prosperity are over and done, you still shall be rich."

After first one — then two — five — and finally seven years, sped quickly by for Nathan, Leah and their sons, God in heaven again summoned Elijah. "Return to earth," he commanded. "See how the couple fare. If they have shown themselves worthy of their blessing, reward them. Otherwise, punish them."

Accordingly, the Prophet once more went down to earth. Disguised as before, as a rich stranger, he visited the village where the couple lived and inquired of a passerby, "Where does the rich man Nathan live?"

The man stared, waved beyond the village, and exclaimed, "Nathan, rich! He lives where he always has, in the field yonder, in the hut where his father and his father's father lived, and he's just as poor. Since he stopped carrying burdens to clear the field, plow the earth, and raise vegetables, Nathan works harder than anyone — and gives more to the poor. It must be his five sons you're thinking of," he added, scratching his head. "*They* prosper — and bright deserving boys they are. Folks say some stranger with gold to spare is interested in them, fancied sending them to school and educating them like princes. Nathan's sons will be learned men."

The disguised Prophet smiled, thanked the man, and hurried to the field. At the door of the humble dwelling he paused and glanced around him. The long straight rows of beans, potatoes and carrots with feathery tops were well tended. The earth was well cultivated. Golden yellow melons hung from sturdy vines. And beside the worn doorstep, tansy, mint and thyme grew lustily. From inside the house came sounds of a woman's singing, a man's laughter, and the tantalizing smell of fresh baking bread.

More pleased than he cared to admit, God's messenger lifted his staff and knocked. But when Nathan opened the door, welcomed him joyfully, and drew him across the threshold, he said gruffly, "I come to warn you, my friend, the good years end tonight. Tomorrow you will be poor, stand in the market square, and seek work, as seven years ago."

"Ah, but the *best* years are ahead," cried Leah, kneeling at the hearth. She now rose quickly, wiped her hands on her apron, and ran forward to greet the stranger. "Thanks to you, kind sir, our sons are prepared to go out into the world, care for themselves and others less fortunate than they. And as for us, we shall never be poor again. Tomorrow is in God's hands, but tonight we are rich," she ended happily. "For you shall break bread with us, we can thank you and tell you of our sons."

"And tonight Leah has a feast," Nathan added proudly. He led the old man to the seat of honor and poured water over his hands. His wife, meanwhile, bustled from hearth to table, dished vegetables from the pot, and poured camel milk from a cracked jar.

The meal that followed was indeed a feast. Nathan's vegetables were tasty with herbs, Leah's barley loaves delicious, and the *leban* — sour milk — was refreshing. And when it came to dessert, no melon was more honey sweet than the fruit Nathan served their guest. "As you see, we fare well," his host said jovially. "With gold for a plow, gold for seed — and plenty of work — the field has yielded an abundance. Besides," he added, looking at his wife, "a fine cook makes good things better!"

To this their guest agreed, ate with relish, and complimented Leah on the meal. Yet he was curious. As he glanced around the mean room, at the simple food and the happy faces, he asked, "During the seven years, haven't you longed for the things riches can buy — a grand house, costly raiment, servants to obey your slightest wish? Aside from educating your sons, and buying a plow and seed for the earth, how else have you spent the gold? How has it changed *your* lives?"

After the shocked silence that followed, Leah spoke first. "But *we* haven't changed!" said she. "We are the same as before. We live in the same way. The only difference is, we have had the joy of giving to the sick and the poor — secretly and through the Rabbi. Only he knew of our wealth. We didn't take the gold for *ourselves*, kind sir," she ended with dignity. "We accepted it — in trust — for our sons, to fit them to lead useful lives."

Then the couple went on to speak of each youth in turn, from the eldest who had passed his examinations to practice medicine, to the youngest, who was studying the Holy Scriptures. "Of all our sons, he has the best mind and the kindest heart," concluded Nathan. "His master says he will be a great rabbi."

The face of the stranger glowed like the sun. "You have shown yourselves worthy, for you have spent the gold wisely, and therefore you shall receive your reward." He rose and bade Nathan and Leah to follow him outside.

And now, the couple clung to each other in fear. For before their eyes their guest grew taller and his face, more radiant, and when he raised his staff, lo! the hovel disappeared. In its place rose a dazzling white palace. Around it were gardens fragrant with flowers, vineyards heavy with red and purple grapes, and an orchard laden with ripe fruit.

As from afar, Nathan and Leah heard the stranger say, "All this is yours. The best years *are* ahead, and from this day God will bless with happiness your goings-out and your comings-in."

"Then you are — you are —" faltered Nathan.

"The Prophet Elijah," replied the Shining One. "God sent me to test you, tempt you with gold and see how you would use it. You have shown yourselves worthy. And now, *shalom aleichem* — peace be with you," he ended and vanished.

Nathan and Leah entered the dazzling white palace hand in hand. And there the pair lived — and after them, their sons and their sons' sons. And of the couple all the folk roundabout said, "No wayfarer knocked in vain at their gate, no beggar left unfed, and on a Sabbath Eve, so long as they lived, a poor man never stood in the marketplace and prayed for work."

THE GRATEFUL ASS   (Egypt)

Young Hasan lived in Cairo with his father, a skilled silversmith. All day the old man sat cross-legged in his tiny shop and fashioned bangles, rings and anklets with their myriads of tinkling bells. And because he was honest, loved his craft, and made objects of rare beauty, his shop prospered.

And Hasan — who loved his father dearly — did his part. Though he had no gift with the hammer and no taste for trade, his gentle manner and handsome face attracted customers — especially the young ladies. Hasan knew which ring — the one with tiny silver balls or the one shaped like a lotus — best suited a slender finger. Even though he could see nothing but the dark eyes of the veiled beauties, he could advise them on the right earrings and prettiest bangles. "When you wait on the ladies, I have more orders to fill than hours in which to fill them," the old man complained, his eyes twinkling.

Despite his skill at pleasing customers, Hasan was so improvident that his father despaired of ever making him a successful owner of a shop. "Money slips through his fingers as if it were water," the old man said, sighing.

For when Hasan had money, he spent it, though not on himself. "It's round — and rolls away," he'd explain with a sheepish grin when he brought home a coarse shirt, striped cotton turban and shoddy sandals, instead of the handsome outfit for which his father had provided a purseful of silver.

What Hasan didn't explain was that he'd spent the money on the gaunt beggar with only one greasy *para* in his bowl, the old market woman who wept because no one bought her flyspecked sweets, and the pilgrim, swaying from hunger at the door of the mosque.

Though Hasan said nothing of all this, others brought word of his son's generosity to the old man, who stroked his beard and thought, *In this world, the lad will never keep anything, but in paradise he'll be rich! The Prophet says, "A man's wealth hereafter depends on his good works on earth."* Just the same, for all his pride in his son's generosity, the father couldn't help wishing that Hasan would consider his own future.

Before long the old man, who was heavy with years, sold his shop and retired. And now more eager than ever to see his son established, he said, "Before I die, I'd like you to wed a beautiful girl, settle in a home of your own, and have a trade."

Hasan placed an arm around his father's shoulders affectionately. "You find the bride, dear Father. I'll find the trade," he told him.

But before Hasan found a trade or the old man a bride, the Angel of Death claimed his father's soul. Hasan inherited his house, five hundred pieces of silver and enough bits of property to live on for a time.

Things went well enough, and the young man took his time about finding a trade. Then, one day, as Hasan was passing the fountain near the bazaar, he noticed a slender young woman who had just filled her water jar. Before lifting it to her shoulder, she glanced around quickly and, seeing no one, stooped to drink from the fountain. It was then her veil dropped accidentally and revealed the most ravishing face — the whitest skin, a perfect small nose and the sweetest lips in the world. Hasan's heart fluttered strangely. And when the maiden hastily rearranged her veil, their eyes met. She blushed deeply, and Hasan knew he was head-over-heels in love!

At once the beautiful creature lifted her jug and hurried toward the poorer quarter of the city. The maiden threaded her way through the narrow winding streets till she came to the door of a humble house, and then disappeared. "She's the only girl I'll ever love," the young man said, sighing as he gazed at the closed door.

Now, knowing where his loved one lived, Hasan lost no time in making inquiries about her from the folk of the neighborhood. Her name was Maima, they said. She lived with her father and supported herself with fine needlework. "She's poor, but good as she is beautiful," they told him. "Her mother died when she was a child, and her father is greedy — so greedy he intends to wed her to a rich man, and demand a sum of money for himself. Maima will make a splendid wife for some lucky young man," they added encouragingly. And now Hasan wished he had established himself.

But thanks to my dear father, I have five hundred pieces of silver, thought Hasan. *That may be enough.* And he promptly called on Maima's father.

When Hasan told of his love for Maima and asked for her hand in marriage, her father received him kindly and seemed to approve the match. The old man called his daughter and bade her serve coffee and sweets. And while the two smiled, gazed into each other's eyes, and whispered pretty nothings, her father busied himself with his water pipe and seemed pleased at the way things were going.

But later, after Maima retired behind a screen and the old man brought up the matter of providing for her — and himself — his attitude changed. For when Hasan said proudly he had inherited from his father a house and five hundred pieces of silver and could take care of her well, the girl's father laughed scornfully. "What! — That paltry sum! What about *me*?" he asked. "Any man who marries my daughter — who has virtue and wit, as well as beauty — must pay *me* for the privilege! A thousand pieces of silver is the amount I require."

"But only a rich man could pay so much!" exclaimed Hasan, blanching.

"My daughter has rich suitors, as well as poor," Maima's father said coldly. "And there is one wealthy man in particular who wishes to wed her. If you love Maima as much as you profess, I daresay you'll find a way to get the sum."

"But I'll need time to raise it," Hasan protested, glancing toward the screen, behind which Maima was sobbing as though her heart would break. "Five hundred pieces of silver are not to be plucked like dates from a palm!"

A greedy smile flitted across the old man's face. "That is your problem. Return with the money within three weeks — unless you wish to see my daughter marry another," he shrugged.

When Hasan took his leave shortly, Maima managed to be at the door. "Never fear, dear love," he whispered, with more confidence than he felt. "I'll be back with the money — in time."

"Don't fail me," sobbed the girl. "He p-plans to marry me to an ugly old man whom I loathe."

In spite of his brave words, Hasan wondered all the way home how he could make good his promise. And once there, he lifted a stone in the floor, took out his inheritance, and counted it. Yet no matter how many times he counted, the amount was always the same!

All night Hasan fretted, twisted, and muttered, "Five hundred pieces of silver stand between me and my happiness!" All night he wondered what to do. It was almost dawn when he thought of his rich Uncle Halim, who lived seven miles distant, at Nagad. Uncle had paid his parents a visit when Hasan was only a baby. However, he recalled his father said once, "Halim is wealthier than a sheikh," then said no more, and so far as the youth knew, the brothers never met again.

But thinking of Uncle Halim now, Hasan had a sudden inspiration. *"He'll* help me!" he cried. "When he knows how much I love Maima, he'll lend five hundred pieces of silver to his only brother's son." Come morning he'd visit his uncle, the youth planned, tell him of his father's death and — Before Hasan decided what else he'd say, he was asleep, a smile on his lips.

It was afternoon, next day, when Hasan turned a bend in the dusty road to Cairo and saw the village of Nagad in a fold of the hill. He was wondering which of the fine houses on the slope above the humble settlement might be his uncle's, when along stumped an aged wood-cutter. "Good day, Father, may Allah give you long life," the youth said politely and asked, "Can you tell me where to find the house of the wealthy Halim?"

"The wealthy Halim, eh? Ha-ha," chortled the man. "It's easy to see you're a stranger. If it's the miserly Halim, who's too mean to share a picked bone with a beggar, you're looking for, he lives yonder, at the far end of the village." And now the man pointed a crooked finger to-ward a tumbledown hovel, with a wretched courtyard and shed.

Hasan's head whirled as he thanked the woodcutter and hurried down the road to knock at the door of the mean dwelling. "Who's there?" rasped a voice from within. "What do you want?" Before

Hasan could reply, the door opened cautiously, and a withered old man with beady eyes and ragged tunic peered at him.

Trying to hide his dismay, the youth faltered, "D-dear Uncle H-Halim, I'm your nephew Hasan, whom you haven't seen these many years. I've come to pay a visit, ask after your health and tell you of your brother's — and my dear father's — death. I should have come sooner," he went on lamely, ashamed of his neglect. "But between my grief and not having seen you since I was a baby —"

But Halim wasn't listening. "Well, well, dear Nephew, welcome," cried the old man. He embraced Hasan and drew him into a dark foul room, with no furnishings save a water jug and two torn mats on the floor. "Alas, for my poor brother. How did it happen? When? I'm well enough, Allah be praised. As you see, I have little to offer by way of hospitality, but all I have is yours," he ended grandly and waved to one of the mats.

Thereupon the old man puttered about for refreshments. How Hasan managed to swallow the supper of moldy bread, rancid goat cheese and stale water set before him, he never knew. And after he'd told of his father's death — and again tried to excuse himself for tardily bringing the news — they chatted of this and that. Halim spoke of his poverty, of life in the village and how cruel and mean people were. "They've cheated, robbed, and swindled me out of the riches I once had," he whined, his eyes glittering strangely.

His father's words "He's wealthier than a sheikh" flashed through Hasan's mind. For an instant he couldn't help wondering how anyone had managed to swindle the sharp-eyed old man. *Unless he really is a miser*, the youth thought.

Dismayed though he was by his uncle's seeming poverty, Hasan decided to tell about his beautiful Maima, about how much he wanted to marry her and about her father's outrageous demands. "All I have are the five hundred silver pieces my dear father left me," the youth said. "To win my bride, I must borrow five hundred more."

"Hmmm-m, she's too expensive for the likes of you," reproved Uncle Halim. "Would I could help you, boy. But as you see, I'm a beggar. All *I* have is a skinny ass in the shed yonder. Tomorrow I'll sell her at the bazaar and get enough, I hope, to keep body and soul together — for a few weeks longer," he ended with a whine.

Hasan choked back his disappointment and chagrin as best he could. Finally he excused himself, saying it was his wont to take a stroll in the air before he retired.

Crossing the courtyard, Hasan passed the shed. And when he saw the small bony beast within, picking dismally at bits of dirty straw, his heart was moved with pity. "You poor starved creature," he exclaimed, as he stroked the long pointed ears and ran a hand over the lean sides. Then seeing the empty water trough, he muttered indignantly, "Your master's too mean to feed himself or you — but he might at least give you water!"

Hasan lost no time in tending the poor beast. He snatched up a bucket, took it to the village font, and drew water. Then he bought barley and straw from a small shop nearby, rushed back to the forlorn ass, and filled her trough and crib. Yet, starved though she was, the animal nuzzled his hand, eyed him gratefully, and then deliberately lifted a foreleg and struck the ground.

Hasan thought no more of the incident until later that night. Stretched uncomfortably on the floor of the hovel, he thought over the disappointing events of the day and tried to decide what to do next. But the longer he fretted and tossed, the more strangely jumbled his mind became. Each time he thought of Maima's lovely face, he seemed to see the pleading eyes of the ass, recalled her odd stamping, and wondered if perchance she wanted to tell him something.

Whether he dozed finally or whether he didn't, Hasan didn't know. But as the hours wore on, his thoughts jumbled yet more. By morning, when he rose stiff and aching in every bone, he was convinced that the fate of the wretched beast outside was linked to Maima's and his.

That was why, when Uncle Halim — who was spry as a cricket and served an even more meager meal than on the previous night — again spoke of the ass and proposed that Hasan accompany him to the bazaar, the youth readily agreed.

But when the old man took Hasan to the shed and he rubbed the beast's back, the small body quivered under his hand. On a sudden impulse, the youth decided to buy her. "How much do you hope to get for such a starved creature?" he asked, trying to sound casual. "Surely, the ass isn't worth more than three pieces of silver?"

"Three pieces of silver, indeed!" Halim snorted, his eyes glittering. "You must think I intend to give away the last thing I own!"

"Seven, eh?" prodded Hasan, rubbing the lean flanks. "The beast is a bag of bones — too scrawny and weak to be of any use," he added. And now the ass turned, gazed at him, and then, as before, stamped on the ground.

Glancing up, Hasan saw Uncle Halim's sharp eyes upon him. "My dear Nephew," he said, "you must think me mad, if you suppose I'd take less than a hundred pieces of silver for such a fine beast."

"*A hundred!*" exclaimed Hasan, his heart sinking. But he added quickly, though he didn't know why, "I'll buy your ass. But since my money is at home, why not accompany me and stay a few days?"

To this the old man agreed, much pleased at the unexpected turn of events.

And now that Hasan had made his foolish decision, his heart was lighter. As he set out for home with the beast and Uncle Halim, a faint hope stirred in the youth's breast. For some unknown reason, he had a feeling things would come right, after all.

And as for the small doleful ass, a change in masters brought about a change in her. All the way to Cairo, she frisked and pranced on the road. And once, in the shade of a palm, she rolled on her back and kicked her heels in joy. Uncle Halim gaped as he leaned on his stick to watch her antics. "I didn't know she had so much life!" he exclaimed.

But Hasan was busy with his own thoughts. *I'll name the little ass Lali*, he planned. *She's young and, with food and care, will be pretty — pretty enough to carry my beautiful Maima, when need be.*

Once at home, Hasan built a stall, lined it with fragrant straw, and gave Lali all the barley and oats she could hold. Then he brushed and groomed her rough coat. "She eats more in a day than I in a month," grumbled Uncle Halim sourly, wishing secretly he'd asked a bigger price. "You'll pamper her so she'll never work."

"And you starved her so she never could!" retorted his nephew.

Despite his grumblings, the old man enjoyed his visit, ate heartily, and after three days announced he'd best get on home, "Before I burst, as yonder beast surely will," he added with a grin. Then he once more counted greedily the hundred pieces of silver he'd received from Hasan, tucked them inside his belt, and took his leave.

After his uncle departed, Hasan soberly faced his financial plight. For now what with six — instead of five hundred pieces of silver — to raise, barely a fortnight to do it, and no prospect of borrowing, he was worse off than before. "Except for you," he told Lali. And when the small creature nudged him gaily, he felt cheered, though why, he couldn't tell.

When word came, three days later, that on Uncle Halim's homeward journey robbers had attacked him, stolen his silver, and left him dead beside the road, Hasan was filled with sadness. "Poor Uncle Halim," he sighed, thinking of his greed and the squalor in which he lived. And then, as his next of kin and heir, the youth set out at once for Nagad. "Not that I'll be likely to find so much as a para," he told Lali, now strong enough to carry her master.

The beast stepped out briskly and with an eagerness that astonished Hasan. "A short time ago, you were overjoyed to leave the place where you suffered such misery. Now you can't wait to return," he said, as the ass broke into a trot.

When they arrived at their destination, the animal's behavior was even more extraordinary. Hasan tied her in her old shed, gave her water and grain, and stepped inside the hovel. But immediately Lali brayed and raised a fearsome commotion. He ran out quickly, thinking something was amiss.

Nothing was — so far as her master could see. When he patted Lali's head, she snorted rudely, nipped at his hand when he held out grain, and when he spoke gently, answered with brays. Then, as before, she struck the earthen floor of the stall with her foreleg.

At his wits' end, Hasan returned to the house. But after the strange goings-on occurred a second, and then a third time, and each time Lali struck the ground more insistently, he decided that perhaps the beast wanted him to dig there in the stall.

When Hasan glanced around, spied a rusty long-handled shovel in the corner, and started to dig, the ass became quiet. With pricked-up ears, nose close to the ground, and a satisfied expression on her face, she watched him turn up the earth. When he paused to wipe sweat from his brow, she impatiently tapped the ground, as though to say, "Don't stop, go on — dig, dig."

And Hasan dug — until the shovel scraped metal. Then he peered inside the hole. And when he saw the end of an old iron-bound coffer, he whooped, "So that's what you've been trying to tell me was hidden here!"

Hasan hauled out the coffer, pried up the lid, and a stream of gold coins poured over the ground. He gaped stupidly. "Truly, Uncle Halim was wealthier than a sheikh, Allah be praised," he mumbled when able to speak. "He was a fraud, a miser. And —" he shouted, leaping to his feet, "you and I are rich, Lali, and I can wed my beautiful Maima." Then he threw his arms about Lali and laughed and cried into her furry neck.

But even now, Lali wasn't satisfied. She yanked herself free from her master's arms, moved a short distance, and struck her foot on the ground in another spot. This time Hasan knew what to do. Once more he snatched up the shovel, dug down deep, and didn't stop until the blade rasped on metal.

Soon Hasan unearthed another chest — a chest smaller, older, and more difficult to open than the first. When at last he pushed back the lid, he stared in astonishment. For in the box lay diamond necklaces, ropes of pearls and ancient rings sparkling with sapphires and rubies. "No queen ever wore such jewels as my Maima shall wear," he whispered.

The following day, when Hasan, attired in costly raiment, knocked at the door of Maima's father, gave him a bag containing a thousand pieces of silver, and once more asked to wed his daughter, the old one's jaw dropped. "But I thought — I thought —" he stammered, staring at the young man's handsome clothes.

"I was poor!" Hasan said with a grin. "And I was — until an old uncle died! But now I'm the richest man in the world," he added, swept Maima into his arms, and pressed her close to his heart.

Three weeks later, when Hasan married the beautiful Maima in the mosque, all the folk of the neighborhood rejoiced. For all knew of the bridegroom's generosity and of the bride's goodness. "The match was made in Paradise," they said. "May Allah bless the pair with happiness and a dozen sons."

And so Allah did. For the longer Hasan and Maima lived — and that was many years, according to the old storytellers — the happier they were, the more tenderly they loved each other, and the more lavishly they gave to the needy and the sick. In time they had sons — twelve in all — who grew tall and straight as the palms on the banks of the Nile.

"It doesn't seem fair," Hasan sighed, thinking of his miserly old uncle. "Giving is such pleasure! Yet poor Uncle Halim never had it. He lived like a beggar, starved himself and his beast, and paid for one hundred pieces of silver with his life!"

For the remainder of her life, Allah blessed the small, faithful beast no less than her master and mistress. "Nothing is too good for Lali. We owe her our happiness," Hasan told his wife. He decked out Lali in a richly striped saddlecloth, bobbing woolen tassels to keep flies away from her eyes, and a dozen strings of blue beads to ward off the Evil Eye.

And each day Lali, dressed in her finery, carried her mistress through

the streets. The little ass advanced daintily, with small mincing steps. And Hasan, walking at her head, patted her sleek neck, glanced back at his wife, and said proudly, "Lali knows she is carrying the most beautiful girl in all Cairo!"

5

THE SEVENTH SON   (Turkey)

Long ago in Turkey, when the sparrow was an informer and the camel a crier in the streets, Allah's servant, the god Zanahari, ruled the destinies of men.

In that far-off time, a man and his sons lived on a prosperous farm high in the hills above the Bosporus. The man's purple figs were the plumpest and his grapes were the sweetest and juiciest and brought the best prices in the marketplace. "I have my sons to thank for my good fortune — especially my seventh, my son Hamid," the father often said, with an arm about the youth's frail shoulders.

Hamid, unlike his six brothers, who were big handsome fellows with broad backs and more brawn than brains, was puny, short of stature and plain of face. Yet Hamid considered himself lucky. For if he'd been strong like the others, he would not have learned to read, write, and do sums in his head. When he was still a child, his father said, "My beloved seventh son, you shall never be able to earn a living with your muscle. Therefore we must see to it that you develop your brain. You must go to the *mullah*'s school in the village. He is judge and priest and a wise teacher. He will teach you to use your brain."

And so it came to pass because Hamid was a willing pupil. He developed a shrewd head, a kind heart, and a humble spirit. Moreover, he was industrious and willing to oversee everything on the farm. As his father grew old and feeble, more and more of these duties fell to Hamid's care. He knew where to spend, where to skimp, and how to sell figs and grapes at the highest prices. The old man increasingly depended on his seventh son.

That was why Hamid's older brothers found fault with him at every turn. "*We* do all the work! While he loafs in the house, we sweat in the sun. We plant, prune, and pick all day, but our father pampers him, for Hamid is certainly his favorite."

His eldest brother, Akit, ridiculed Hamid most. One day in the village square, when Hamid's eyes wistfully followed the graceful figure of the lovely veiled Leyla, who was filling her jar at the font along with the other maidens, Akit sneered meanly. And his father, scuffing ahead in upturned slippers, overheard the unkind remark. "Ho, ho, little brother," his firstborn was saying, "no girl would fall in love with a man so ugly and short — even though her father arranged the match with an eye to business!"

Hamid, as usual, smiled and said nothing, though he couldn't help wishing his brother were kinder. But that night his father, sitting beside the brazier with his bubbling water pipe, sent for Akit and sternly reproved him. "For shame, my son," said the old man, his long mustachios trembling in anger. "Handsome is as handsome does! Because you *happen* to be tall and are so handsome many a veiled beauty turns a head when you pass, that is no reason for you to sneer at your youngest brother. One day the father of the prettiest girl in the village will be glad to have Hamid wed his daughter for what he *is*, not what he seems!"

On the First Day of the First Moon, *Muharram* — the Feast of the New Year — the old man gave each son a gold piece, a vest trimmed with real gold braid and a blessing, saying, "May Allah guard you well." And they fared well indeed. Thrice each week the servant set before them a dish of mutton and rice, together with meat broth and bread. On feast days, there was extra *baklava* — layers of pastry put together with ground nuts and honey — and tobacco to smoke. And when they jogged to market, enough extra *kurus* jingled in their purses for any number of cups of sweet thick black coffee.

"We fare better than other farmers' sons," Hamid reminded his brothers when they complained of how hard they worked. "At least, we have plenty to show for our labors."

"You mean *you* do!" retorted the second eldest brother, Murad.

"You hoodwink our father into thinking you work harder than anyone."

Hamid bit his tongue and held his peace. *They are so handsome and big, it's no wonder they are impatient with a little fellow like me,* he thought, excusing them. Yet, despite his brothers' scorn, he was content enough. He loved his father and also the land. To manage it wisely and see it yield was enough to rejoice his heart.

But one day, when his father was stricken with a fever, Hamid's life changed suddenly. "My sons, I have not long to live," the old man weakly told the youths. "The farm is your inheritance and belongs to all of you equally. And so — so do the contents of yonder strongbox. Hamid has the key. You, Akit, as the eldest, shall head this house," he gasped. "And Hamid is to manage everything." And with these words he died.

After the forty days and forty nights of mourning, Akit donned his brightest vest and fez, swaggered about like a pasha and ordered his brothers to do this and that. "And as for you, little brother," he told Hamid one day ,"your time of loafing is over. From now on, you'll work for your bread!"

"But I do, though not with my hands," said Hamid, drawing up his short figure with dignity. "Besides, our father wished —"

"Our father is dead," interrupted Akit. "I head this house, as you'll do well to remember. And while we're about it, hand over our father's strongbox."

Hamid didn't argue. He was no match for this burly brother, who set him to work at tasks far beyond his strength and jeered at him without ceasing. "Much good *you* are on this farm!" Akit said over and over. And the other brothers, following his lead, laughed and added their share to making Hamid's life wretched.

Yet his brothers' sloth, their wanton waste, and their neglect of the land hurt Hamid even more than their unkindness. "If only I were a big man, I could make them listen to me," he cried one night as he tossed on his bed, muscles sore and bones aching. "In another six months the farm will be ruined."

Whether Hamid drifted into sleep while wondering what to do next, or whether he didn't, he couldn't tell. But all at once, he was sitting bolt upright in bed, his spine tingling with excitement. For now an idea whirled through his mind like a dervish — an idea so splendid he pinched himself to make sure he was awake.

"That's it! That's what I'll do this very night — *now*," Hamid cried. "I'll go seek the god Zanahari. Our beloved father used to say, 'Allah's servant often helps mortals in need — mortals who seek him in humility and make a wish.' I'll ask Zanahari to make me big and strong."

Hamid pulled on his clothes and crept out through the door, into the moonlight. Then he hurried away as fast as his short legs would carry him.

At the crossroads, Hamid stopped and tried to decide which way to

go. To the east lay a dense forest; a path zigzagged to the west; and straight ahead, a steep mountain rose from a rough meadow.

While Hamid peered this way and that, a thin voice behind him said, "Who are you, young man, and where are you going?"

Hamid whirled around. Standing in the moonlight was a wizened old man with a long white beard, voluminous green silk trousers, and green turban, fastened with a diamond as big as a star. "I — I'm Hamid," the youth faltered. "I set out to find the god Zanahari, but having reached the crossroads, I don't know which way to go. Can you tell me?" he mustered courage to ask.

The man in the turban stared at the youth. "Zanahari, eh?" he muttered. "What, pray, do you want with him?"

"I want him to make me as big and strong as my brothers," said Hamid. "It's not that I'm vain," he went on quickly. "But if I'm to save our father's land, I've got to be strong. I'm too small now to do anything," he ended dismally.

Then before he knew it, he was pouring out the story of his father's death, his brothers' scorn, and how he had vainly tried to do tasks that proved too much for his size and strength. It wasn't that Akit and the others *meant* to be unkind, he took care to explain. "It's because I'm puny. They can't understand that it takes a head, as well as a strong back, to raise grapes and figs such as ours. And being so handsome and big themselves, they refuse to take advice from one so small."

The old man pulled at his beard, regarded Hamid thoughtfully, and when he spoke, his voice was kind. "I'll tell you how to find Zanahari. If you do as I say, tell him your troubles, and ask his help, you have naught to fear. But if you don't —" he added, eyes flashing.

"But I *shall*," interrupted Hamid. "Please, kind **Father**, tell me what to do."

"Then listen well," the Old One said. "You will journey three days and three nights to reach Zanahari's dwelling. The way is hard. You shall endure thirst, hunger, and weariness. But heed these words, lest you incur the god's displeasure and lose all," he warned, fixing bright eyes on Hamid's face.

The man in the turban pointed to the meadow and said, "Go straight ahead, climb yonder mountain, and descend the far side. You shall reach an orange grove of seven trees. Each tree bears a single orange — round, golden and thrice the size of your head. On no account gaze at the fruit, tarry, or pick it. The land, the grove and the oranges belong to Zanahari."

"But I would not pick fruit that is another's," said Hamid.

" 'Tis well," the Old One nodded. "The second day of your journey you will reach a broad meadow with a stream and rocks over which kids and goats frisk. Do not linger beside the stream, throw stones at the kids, or frighten them. They belong to Zanahari."

"But I'd not harm or frighten helpless beasts," Hamid assured him.

"And lucky for you!" the man in the green turban replied, the great diamond glittering in the moolight. "After a journey of another night, you'll hear waters burbling, and you will see a spring, cold and clear, gushing from rocks. You will long to drink. But taste not the water. It is Zanahari's. Hasten on. On the morning of the third day you will see his fine white palace rising in the distance."

"Ahh-h," Hamid sighed, clasping his hands.

But the old man had not finished. "Go to the door, knock, and respectfully salaam to the beautiful young woman who greets you. She is Zanahari's wife. The god will be absent, but she will offer you a jug of wine. Accept her hospitality, drink the wine, but do not touch the jug."

"I shall do as you say," Hamid promised, though he couldn't think how to drink without touching the jug. "And Zanahari — when shall I see him?"

"When he returns," the Old One said. "He will ask your wish, ask about your journey, and then if you have heeded my words, all will be well and Allah the Good will bless you."

The old man spoke so kindly that hope stirred in Hamid's breast. But before the youth could thank him, the Old One vanished.

Hamid set out at once for the mountain. He soon discovered the distance was greater than he had supposed, the grasses were higher, and his legs so short that he stumbled over stones and rocks. Still, his courage didn't flag. When forced to stop to catch his breath, the youth whispered, "Zanahari will help me," and when he started on, his limbs felt stronger.

How he reached the mountain, climbed over it and descended the far side, the youth didn't know. Nor could he recall, later, where he slept — if sleep he did — or what food he found on the way. The sun was shining when he reached the orange grove the Old One had described. And there from the branches hung the huge golden oranges. Hamid longed to taste one. But mindful of his instructions, he hurried on.

The next day the youth reached the field. There goats and kids gamboled beside a stream that flowed like a ribbon through the flower-spangled meadow. "What beautiful creatures!" he said, smiling at their droll antics. "Whoever would harm Zanahari's kids?" And weary though he was, and much as he longed to drink and bathe in the cool water, he plodded on.

How Hamid endured the tortures of hunger, weakness and thirst that assailed him the third night and day of his journey is difficult to imagine. But endure them he did. When at last he heard the sound of gushing waters and saw them spill over the rocks, his lips were so parched that he could scarcely form the words, "What crystal clear — water — belongs to Zanahari."

After a long time — or a short time— Hamid couldn't tell which, he stood at the door of the god's fine white palace. He swayed giddily as he knocked. But when a beautiful young woman opened the door, he salaamed before her. When he rose, so weak he could scarcely stand, she offered him wine and held the jug toward him.

And thirsty though he was, Hamid remembered the Old One's words in time. In that moment of agony, he knew what to do. "Thank you, kind mistress," he gasped. "Please pour the wine down my throat." And he opened his mouth.

The wine made Hamid feel strangely refreshed. Once more he salaamed before Zanahari's wife and said gratefully, "Thank you for saving my life."

At that moment Zanahari returned home and demanded, "Who are you, little man? Whence do you come, and what is your wish?"

The youth fell to his knees and touched his forehead thrice to the floor. Then, summoning up all his courage, he said, "My name is Hamid. I come from a faraway farm in a faraway village — a journey of three days and three nights. My wish is to be big and strong." Swallowing hard, he continued, "I am so puny and small I cannot work to save the land our beloved father left my brothers and me, or make them heed me when I tell them to plant, prune, or — or —" he floundered, all at once too overcome by his own presumption to look at the god.

And so Hamid did not see the kindness in Zanahari's face, the light in his eyes, or the smile on his lips when he asked abruptly, "On the way thither, little man, did you see my oranges?"

"Yes, Zanahari, I saw your marvelous oranges, but I did not touch them," replied Hamid.

"Hmmm-m, and did you see my herd of kids and goats?" the god asked.

"Yes, and they are beautiful creatures," said Hamid, hastening to add, "But I did not harm them, tarry in the field, or linger by the stream."

"And my spring — did you drink the water?" questioned Zanahari.

"No, though I nigh fainted from thirst, I did not drink of your water," Hamid said.

Zanahari nodded approval, stroked his beard, and turned to his wife. "Was the little man polite when you offered him wine, dear love? Did he treat you as becomes my wife?"

"Yes, lord," replied Zanahari's wife, with an encouraging smile at Hamid. "He thanked me, salaamed, and begged me to pour the wine down his throat."

"Without touching the jug, dear one?" Zanahari pursued.

"Without so much as brushing it with a fingertip, lord," the young woman assured him.

Now the god's face shone as the sun. "Then all is well, young man. You shall have your wish, and Allah be praised," he said, and placed a hand on Hamid's head.

In that instant, a sense of well-being such as he had never known flowed through Hamid's small body. He felt himself grow taller, and strength flowed through his weak limbs. As if in a dream, he heard Zanahari say, "Because you have shown yourself worthy and have come to me in humility, your wish is granted. You shall be tall as your brothers, as handsome of face, and seven times stronger than they."

And now Hamid felt himself being lifted and carried through the air, as on invisible wings. Then he was back in his native village. Overhead the stars twinkled, the moon shone brightly, and he bounded up the slope to the farm in long easy strides.

At the door Hamid paused to listen to the loud wranglings that poured into the night.

"I tell you, there's not so much as a kurus in the chest," Akit blustered.

"And why not?" shouted Murad. "What have you done with the money our father left us?"

And now the next to the youngest brother, Bobo, accused, "You've spent it on yourself, eh, Akit? That's why we've eaten like beggars, gone shabby, and never had enough for a new tunic or a pair of boots!"

"I — I don't know where the money went," Akit whined in a frightened voice. "It just disappeared!"

Hamid pushed the door open, strode into the room, and regarded his brothers with flashing eyes. They in turn gaped, stared, and demanded to know who he was. For among the six, not one recognized, in the tall handsome stranger, the plain puny Hamid.

"I am your youngest brother," the new Hamid announced. Then he flexed his great muscles and grinned at the consternation in the faces before him. "And since I am big, and even stronger than you, I'd advise you not to bully me."

"W — what's happened to you?" Akit wanted to know when he was able to speak. And the others, thinking their brother had returned to avenge himself, cringed, begged forgiveness for their meanness, and fell in fright to their knees.

"Get up, you fools, and listen to me," Hamid ordered, enjoying himself hugely. "When I was weak and small, you refused to do so." He went on to say that henceforth he, Hamid, would manage the farm and that they would share everything equally, *"As our father wished,"* he reminded them. "With hard work, diligence and Allah's help, we can once more make the land yield abundantly." Then turning to Akit, he warned, "You, as the eldest, are head of the house. But those who eat must also work. Tomorrow at dawn we shall start to prune the vines."

And now, though the brothers murmured among themselves, they had no choice but to agree — or pretend to agree — to Hamid's proposal. For what with his powerful body, the ring of authority in his voice and the gleam in his eye, they feared him. Akit handed his brother the key to the empty chest and said, smiling falsely, "You'll see, we'll work hard to make up for the past. And now tell us from start to finish of the miracle that has transformed a small wispy fellow into such a tall handsome man."

Nothing loath, Hamid related his adventure, starting with his resolution to seek out Zanahari and to implore his help. He spoke of the man in the green turban he had met at the crossroads, of the instructions he had received, and his journey to the god's dwelling. "Had I disobeyed the Old One, all would have been lost," he said, telling of Zanahari's questions before he had performed his miracle.

"And here I am as you see me," Hamid ended happily, glancing around at his brothers. Then, reminding them once more that they would start work come morning, he bade them good-night.

Long after he retired, Hamid heard the low rumble of his brothers' voices. "They have plans of their own," he guessed shrewdly, feigned mighty snores, and tried to hear what they said.

Before long, Akit whispered, "If Zanahari could make our puny brother a big handsome man, he could transform *us* — who are already handsome and tall — into giants."

"Giants, ha!" cried Bobo with a pleased squeal. "Then we'd be mightier than men! We would never have to prune or plant — or take orders from Hamid."

"Psss-st! You'll waken the fool!" Akit growled. Then he unfolded his scheme. "Hamid isn't the only one who can play a clever trick. What say, dear brothers, *we* go to the crossroads, find the man in the turban, and ask him what to do? Then we'll seek the god, make *our* wish, and see who has the last laugh!" he ended triumphantly.

Muffled sniggers and exclamations of approval followed. Then Hamid heard the latch lift, stealthy footsteps and the door close softly. "May they have wisdom to follow the Old One's warning," he said, sighing, thinking of the searching questions Zanahari would ask them.

But the brothers, meanwhile, were running down the slope with shouts and guffaws. They raced through the village and, when they reached the crossroads, all but knocked from his feet the old man in the green turban.

"Where are you going in such a hurry?" he asked dryly.

"Ho, ho, to see Zanahari," boomed Akit, speaking for all. "Tell us where to find him, old man, and we'll be on our way."

A malicious smile flitted across the Old One's lips. "What do you want with Zanahari?" he asked.

"We want to be giants," declared Akit.

"Giants, eh?" the old man muttered, pulling at his beard. Then, without further ado, he gave the brothers the same directions and warnings he had given Hamid. But to these the six brothers paid no attention and loped away toward the mountain, with not so much as a thank you to the old man.

Three nights and three days later, when Akit and his brothers appeared before Zanahari — without even bowing their heads — his brow darkened, and he asked coldly, "What is your wish?"

"We want to be giants, the mightiest fellows on earth," announced Akit.

As with Hamid, the god began at once to question the brothers. "On the way here, did you see my orange grove?" he asked.

"Ahhh-h, indeed!" Akit nodded. "Never did we eat such fruit."

Zanahari's eyes smoldered with wrath. "Did you see my kids in the meadow?" he demanded.

"They were better than the oranges!" Akit said with an insolent wink. "We killed three kids and had an excellent meal of them."

"And my spring — did you touch my sacred waters?" Zanahari roared, trembling with rage.

"We drank our fill, bathed our faces and cooled our hands," said Akit. And then, all at once aware of the god's displeasure, he asked sullenly, "Well, water is free and meant to be enjoyed, isn't it?"

Without replying, Zanahari summoned his wife. "How did these ruffians treat you?" asked the god.

"As a slave, lord," the young woman replied, not lifting her eyes. "They ordered wine before I offered it, snatched the jug from my hands, and passed it from one to another, snorting like swine."

Zanahari blanched in anger, rose from his throne, and commanded the young men to come forward. And they, thinking they were about to receive their wish, pushed forward like stupid oafs, with nudges and grins.

Too late, they realized their awful mistake. And the next moment, when Zanahari pronounced his awful judgment, the grins and nudges turned into howls of despair.

For now the god thundered, "Scoundrels — rascals — thieves! You don't deserve to be men, much less giants. You have acted like swine — stealing my oranges, killing my kids, and drinking my water. Worst of all, you have insulted my wife. Henceforth you shall *be* swine, banished to the mountains. There you shall roam wild, despised, hunted, and devoured by men."

"No, no!" shrieked Akit, groveling in horror before the god.

"Not *swine!*" the other brothers screamed and cowered on their knees, faces in hands.

Zanahari paid no heed to the their wild clamorings. Instead, he raised a hand, touched each brother in turn, and lo! they began to change. The six tall handsome young men became six squealing pigs — with bristly backs and small mean eyes. And when the god bellowed, "Begone!" they stampeded to the door. Snorting and screaming, they fled over a field, up a slope, and disappeared in a densely wooded mountainside.

As for Hamid, *he* never learned the fate of his brothers. But as time passed and they never returned, he was sorely troubled. "They disobeyed the Old One, offended the great Zanahari, and he has punished them," he concluded sadly.

And now Hamid prospered, and so did the farm. For what with his size and strength, his knowledge and skill — and plenty of work — in time he coaxed the neglected earth to yield again. The vines bore

sweeter grapes, and the trees plumper figs, than in his father's day.

And the villagers, who had always liked Hamid, watched and rejoiced in his prosperity. "His body has changed, but not his heart," they said. "Good fortune has not spoiled the old man's seventh son."

Summer passed, and so did autumn. Then one day, pleased with the harvest he'd gathered, Hamid decided to ask the father of the beautiful Leyla for his daughter's hand. "I have loved her long — ever since I saw her at the fountain with the other maidens," the youth confessed shyly. "But when I was small, weak and plain of face, I did not have courage to ask you to let me marry her."

"And now you do!" said the old man, eyes twinkling and arm about the young man's broad shoulders. "You have my permission to wed my daughter — though I might have granted it anyway, if you had asked!" Then the father called Leyla.

And in the course of that meeting, the beautiful girl told the handsome young man she was to wed, "I loved you, dear one, from the moment I first set eyes on your kind face."

"My beloved father said I'd marry the prettiest girl in the village, but I didn't believe him!" cried Hamid, sweeping Leyla into his arms.

And so Hamid and Leyla were married and lived happily ever after, blessed with strong handsome sons and beautiful daughters.

6

THE CRIMSON PURSE
AND THE TALKING RAVEN (Iraq)

Ages ago in Babylon — the country now called Iraq — a rich man and his two sons lived on fertile lands somewhere west of Baghdad. Though this man had broad acres, many cattle and the best vineyards anywhere, the youths, Zvi and Zakho, were the light of his soul. "A man's greatest wealth is in his sons," he said proudly, looking from one to the other.

Now both Zvi and Zakho were handsome, stalwart young men. At first glance they looked like two peas, save that Zvi, being older, was taller and broader. Yet there all resemblance ended. For Zvi was greedy, envious by nature, and jealous of his younger brother.

Zakho, on the other hand, was generous to a fault. When he strode through the bazaar, he gave alms freely, chatted with widows, and helped the halt and the blind. "There's not a mean bone in his body," the villagers declared.

But when Zvi swept through the market place, nose in air, he didn't so much as acknowledge the salaams of humble folk. He never dropped a copper into an outstretched hand or helped an old one over the road. "He'd steal coins from a dead man's lids!" sneered the poor.

Thinking of Zvi, his father sighed. He loved this son, despite his greed, and treated both young men with affection. After their dear mother had died, the good man tried to rear them sensibly. He taught them to plow, trim vines, and tend the beasts. "A good master is first a good farmer," he told them.

Yet as time passed and the father grew older, he was uneasy lest Zakho fare badly after his death. For Zvi — though he'd recently wed the beauteous Lea and brought her home to his father's roof — was more grasping than ever — and his wife more so than he.

That was why the father summoned the brothers, one day, and said, "Dear sons, I find you both capable, love you both dearly — neither one more nor the other less. Therefore I have decided to divide my possessions between you. The day I die, dear Zvi, you shall receive half my fields, vinelands and beasts, and you, dear Zakho, the other half."

"Oh, thank you, thank you, dear Father," cried Zakho, the younger, his eyes like stars. "I shall strive to be worthy of your trust, and may the day of your death be distant."

An Zvi, though secretly furious, forced himself to say, "You are indeed generous to your sons." Then he begged his father to excuse him,

as he had work elsewhere, and went to seek Lea. "The old man is mad
and in his dotage," he shouted. "To think I'm to share equally with a
young puppy who isn't yet dry behind the ears! Custom demands that I,
Zvi, as the firstborn, inherit all and dole out what I see fit to my
younger brother."

"And so you shall, dear husband — if you do as I say," Lea purred,
as an evil scheme crept into her mind. But when her husband stared
and inquired what she had in that pretty head, she laughed softly and
twined white arms around his neck. "Your father is old," she whispered.
"It won't be long now — and when the time comes, I have a plan."

But when Zvi inquired what the plan might be, all she replied was,
"Wait and see," a crafty smile on her lovely lips.

Zvi waited with all-concealed impatience, until one day strange
giddiness seized his father. The old man took to his bed, never to
rise again. Sometime later, he beckoned his sons to come close. "Dear
sons," he whispered as they bent over him, "my end is near . . . remember my wish. Divide everything — share all equally — "

Zakho's eyes filled with tears. "We'll remember, dear Father," he
said as the pale lids fluttered and the weak voice drifted away.

"As if we could forget!" Zvi sneered and turned quickly to hide
the greed that filled his eyes.

And now when Zvi returned to Lea, she again advised patience.
"Wait until the mourning ends — the hymns are chanted, the sacrifices
made and the wise men have consulted the stars," she said. "Then go

to Zakho, show brotherly concern, and tell him it's time to divide the properties as your father desired. Then propose a plowing contest."

"A plowing contest!" Zvi exclaimed. "At plowing, Zakho always wins!"

"Not this time. This time he'll lose," Lea said slyly and then unfolded her evil scheme — a scheme to rob Zakho of his inheritance.

When Lea was done, Zvi laughed boisterously. "Ho, ho, what a wife!" he cried and swept her into his arms and promised more shimmering veils and pretty bangles than any girl possessed.

When Zvi later went to Zakho, the youth was pacing the courtyard with shoulders drooping and downcast eyes. "Come, come, dear Brother," said Zvi, feigning sympathy. "The time of mourning is past, the gods have had their way. Our father has reached the Cavern of the Dead, and our tears cannot recall him. Now we must carry out his wishes and divide the property. Tomorrow we must decide which lands are yours, which mine."

"Take what you like, but leave me now," Zakho replied without glancing up. "I'm not ready to make decisions yet."

"Ah, dear Brother, I understand," Zvi said so smoothly that Zakho glanced up quickly. "I want to help you, discuss a plan that will save you from making decisions — and solve everything."

When Zakho saw the avarice in Zvi's eyes and the crafty smile on his lips, he had an uneasy feeling that the plan boded no good. "What is it?" he asked coldly.

But Zvi — who didn't notice that Zakho was staring as though seeing him for the first time— gleefully rubbed his hands and cried, "My plan is a plowing match, dear Brother, between you and me! We'll rise tomorrow before dawn, agree to eat and drink nothing, and go out to plow. That way, we can see who plows the most ground in a day and decide —"

"Decide *what?*" demanded Zakho. "At plowing you have never distinguished yourself!"

Striving to keep his temper, Zvi said smoothly, "Decide which brother wins all and remains as the rightful master, and which one loses and leaves — emptyhanded."

"Call me at dawn," his brother said wearily, and resumed his melancholy pacing. For it was clear Zvi intended to swindle him.

The next day the moon was yet high, Zakho asleep, and the house still when Lea rose stealthily. She lighted a fire, prepared a hearty meal, and called Zvi. "Eat well, dear husband," she whispered, dishing out meat and rice and pouring red wine. "To outplow Zakho will take strength."

"Before he collapses from exhaustion and hunger, ha-ha!" chortled Zvi, shaking with silent mirth. "My honest brother will never think of anything as simple as this trick."

It was still dark, Zvi's stomach full, and he in jovial spirits when he shook Zakho's shoulder. "Up, sluggard, up," he boomed. "It's time to rise and put hand to plow."

"Time to rise, eh?" Zakho muttered sleepily. Then, as the events of the previous day rushed back, he jumped from bed, dressed hastily, and followed his brother to the plowlands.

And by now Zvi, pleased at the way things were going, strutted, acted as though he already were the master, and shouted, "You take that side of the field, dear Brother, I'll take this, and we'll see who reaches the center of the field first."

So we shall, Zakho thought uneasily. For though he stepped out briskly, plowed furrow after furrow with his accustomed swiftness and skill — and gained steadily — he had no doubt from the first about who would come out ahead. *Zvi will win*, his brother thought as he watched him wrench the plow, wobble the share this way and that, and fall behind, row after row.

But that was before sunrise. When the burning rays beat down on his back, first hunger and then weakness overcame Zakho. For he had fasted much and slept little while mourning for his father. Toward noon the plow grew strangely heavy, his pace slackened, and at last, he could hardly drag one foot after the other. Sometime later, he sank to his knees, fell in the furrow and blackness swirled over his head.

How long Zakho lay on the ground he didn't know. But after what seemed a year — or a hundred — he felt water on his face and heard Zvi cackle, "Wake up, you fool. You've fainted, I've won the plowing match and now, ha-ha —"

"I'll go," said Zakho, struggling to open his eyes.

When Zakho left his brother's house, he took naught save the garments on his back, the staff in his hand, and a small crimson silk purse that had belonged to his father. *It will bring me luck,* thought the youth, smoothing the bright embroidered thing 'twixt forefinger and thumb. *I remember when, as a lad, I scraped my knee or bumped my head and wanted to cry, dear Father showed me this, let me touch it, and said, "Be brave, little son, this pain will pass"* — and somehow it did! Zakho smiled tenderly at the crimson silk purse.

Whether the purse — or thinking of his father — made Zakho brave now, he didn't know. But no sooner had he tucked the crimson purse inside his belt, stepped out briskly, and said, "The past is past, the future ahead, and there's no time for despair," than he felt a great surge of courage. He planned eagerly, "I'll journey north and find a village close to a forest. Where there are trees, there's work for a young man with a stout heart and the need to earn bread."

And now that his mind was made up, Zakho felt easier and was surprised, a short time later, to find himself whistling.

Toward sunset, he reached a hamlet with sun-dried brick walls and small houses with flat roofs and arched doorways. It was a friendly-looking place, set like a jewel amid rolling hills and emerald pastures. And when he saw the deep forest beside the village, and beyond it the tall mountain glittering like gold in the last rays of the sun, he shouted for joy. "The purse *has* brought me luck! Here's where I'll tarry, build a hut, and live the life of a woodcutter."

And this Zakho did. He worked from dawn to dark, felling trees and selling wood. Few coins ever jingled in his crimson purse, and he was often bone-tired. Yet he was content in his new life.

"A kinder youth never lived," said the villagers, who took an instant liking to the youth. "Though he has little to give the beggar at the door, he gives what he has with a smile worth more than gold."

One day, when as usual Zakho shouldered his ax and went to the forest, he came upon a tree he'd not seen before. It was sturdy and tall, with spreading branches and smooth grayish bark. From the first, there seemed something strange about the tree, though he didn't know what. All he knew was that here was a find, the wood was rare and it would fetch a fancy price at market.

Zakho had just spit on his palms, lifted his ax, and nicked a chopping line around the trunk, when something astonishing occurred. Out from the topmost branches flapped a Raven, with black shining wings and beady black eyes. The bird circled above the tree thrice and then croaked in a human voice, "Spare my helpless nestlings, Woodsman, spare my tree and the home I've built stick by stick, woven with care and lined with eiderdown. You'll not regret it if you do." The Raven swooped to a nearby branch and knowingly cocked her head. "If you show me and mine this kindness, Woodsman, I shall take you to the Mountain of the Sun."

Now Zakho — who'd never heard of the Mountain of the Sun, much less of a talking bird — gaped stupidly. "I— I'll not hurt your nestlings or harm your tree, Raven. But why should I want to go to the M-mountain?" he stammered out at last.

The bird's eyes glittered like black diamonds. "Don't ask silly questions," she said testily. "Return before dawn tomorrow, bring a small

bag, and you'll find out why." Then, without further ado, she darted
back to her nest and disappeared amid the leaves.

That night Zakho was too excited to eat his clabbered milk and bread,
and when he went to bed, he couldn't sleep. The events of the day were
strangely jumbled in his mind. "Bring a small bag," the bird had said.
He'd take the little crimson silk purse, he decided. Thinking of the
purse then reminded him of his father and of a tale he'd told long ago.
There was a talking bird in that — yes, and a mountain, he recalled,
everything fuzzing together. Just before the youth drifted into slumber,
he heard his father saying, "Lucky is the man, my son, who meets the
Raven, goes to the mountain and has no greed in his heart."

When Zakho awoke with a start, it was dark. Fearful lest he be late,
he leaped from bed, pulled on his garments, and ran through the forest,
clutching the purse in one hand. The Raven was already waiting. "Hast-
en and follow me," she said. "We've no time to lose." Spreading her
dark wings, she flew before him.

How Zakho made the journey he never knew, for the distance was
far and the way rough. And when he reached the mountainside,
that was slippery and so steep that for each step forward, he slid back
three. When at last he reached the peak, the Raven dropped to earth,
flapped her wings and said, "Behold the treasure!" Then she pecked
at the earth.

Instantly the mountain opened, and Zakho gasped, for at his feet lay
a treasure such as no other man had seen. There were shining nuggets

of gold, diamonds that sparkled and winked like a hundred-thousand stars, piles of rubies, and heaps of pearls as bright as moonshine.

But now the Raven was saying, "Take your fill, whatever you fancy — *but hurry!* If you linger and the sun rises and finds you here, you shall die. The fierce rays will scorch your back and burn your body to ash." Then she rose swiftly and vanished in the gray shroudlike sky.

Zakho sank to his knees before the glittering jewels, stuffed the small crimson bag with diamonds and rubies, and pulled the drawstring at the top. Then, snatching a lump of gold, he left the cavern.

Zakho wasn't sure what happened next. But when he opened his eyes, he was home on his bed and bright sunlight filtered through the slit of a window in his little square house. At first he thought he'd dreamed the strange adventure. But when he glanced toward the floor, saw the gold nugget and the purse — bulging as never before — he sat bolt upright and whooped, "Ho, ho, it's all *real!* Dear Father was right, and I'm a lucky man!"

Yet despite the realness of the adventure — to say nothing of the treasure — when Zakho went to the forest to thank the Raven, he never found the bird or her tree. "It was magic — that's what it was," he decided and scratched his head in puzzlement.

But now — what with gold and gems — Zakho was rich. The youth promptly built a fine house, surrounded by pastures and fields. Now he raised the fattest cows, the wooliest sheep and the prettiest white frisking lambs anywhere. And though tongues wagged and folks wondered

— and some dared ask — how a poor woodcutter suddenly became so rich, Zakho only rubbed his hands gleefully. "I had an unexpected windfall," he replied, and chuckled as though over some secret joke.

Yet the people didn't begrudge Zakho his good fortune — no, indeed! "No one deserves it more," the villagers agreed. "When he had little, he shared what he had. Now he's rich, he feeds the poor and looks after the sick, seven villages around."

There are many who say only bad news travels fast. This, *we* know is nonsense! Good news also travels fast — especially when it concerns a man like Zakho, who spent more on others than on himself.

Before long, word of his prosperity and good works reached Zvi's ears. "WHAT! A silly fool witless enough to lose his inheritance, rich, swaggering round like a lord and squandering substance on the poor!" he shouted, when Lea rushed home from the bazaar with the astonishing gossip. "But how — *how?*"

"Why don't you find out, dear husband?" asked Lea, through whose mind wily thoughts were already darting. "Why not pay your brother a visit, feign sorrow for the past and then — "

"Worm out his secret and profit by it!" Zvi laughed, rubbing his greedy hands. "Anything *that* simpleton can do, *we* can do better!"

When Zvi returned three days later from his visit, it was easy to tell he'd been successful. "Things went even better than I'd hoped," he boasted. "Thanks to my cleverness, we'll soon be richer than Zakho.

You'll have more jewels than any queen and I more turbans than His Majesty, the Shah!"

Zakho had received him kindly, entertained him as a prince, and bore no grudge, fool that he was. "But I was too smart for him. I'd not go till he spilled the tale of how he'd come by his riches." Zvi chuckled — and started to describe his visit from the beginning. "When he told of the talking raven in the forest who guided him to the mountain and showed him the treasure, I took my leave and — "

"Went to the forest yourself, clever fox!" His wife beamed upon him.

"You're exactly right," Zvi said, flushing with pleasure at Lea's praise. "I went, found the tree, and threw stones. And when the wretched bird appeared and begged me to spare her young, I threatened to kill them all — unless she took *me* to the treasure, that is." Zvi laughed cruelly before concluding, "The Raven didn't dare refuse me. But she glared balefully enough, hopped up and down a branch, and croaked, 'Return before dawn two days hence, bring a small bag and I'll take you there.' A small bag indeed! Bring me three bags, dear wife."

Then he ordered Lea to fetch three empty grain sacks, said time was short and they had work to do before dawn.

As night wore on, the couple bent their heads over the sacks — pulling out seams and stitching the three sacks together to make one huge bag. "Wait till I haul it back full of diamonds and gold, dear wife," gloated Zvi.

And now the couple burst into gales of laughter, smoothed out the great sack, and hugged each other. As the first rays of pink tinged the sky, their task was done — even to the stout string at the top. Zvi took leave of his wife. "I'll be back soon, dear one," he promised. "And soon — what with more diamonds in your hair, pearls round your throat and jewels on your fingers than a queen — you'll be the most beautiful girl in the world." Then he hurried away, dragging the sack at his heels.

The journey to the Mountain of the Sun took place as with Zakho. Zvi struggled to the top. But when the bird alighted and rasped her warning, her voice sounded spiteful and her beady black eyes burned with vengeful light. "Hurry — lest you burn to death and never return," she croaked, flapped away noisily and disappeared in the gray sky.

Zvi — his eyes bulging with greed at sight of the treasure — didn't hear the rasping croak or see the vengeful light in the Raven's eyes. All *he* saw was the glittering gold, the heaped-up diamonds and pearls, the rubies that glowed as richly red as pigeon's blood. He reached out greedy fingers, raked the jewels toward him, and dropped them by handfuls into the mouth of the great yawning sack.

Zvi was still raking gems when the sun rose. As the morning sun broke over the mountainside, folks in the valley below heard shrieks and screams, followed by a long, agonized wail. Then they saw a black raven. "She seemed to rise from nowhere," they reported. "She floated above the mountain and croaked dismally, 'I told you so! *I told you so!* I TOLD YOU SO-OO!'" After that, the bird vanished and no one in those parts saw her again.

Some who tell this tale say that when Zvi didn't return with the gold and jewels he'd promised, Lea went mad with disappointment and rage. Others claim she soon lost the riches she'd schemed and connived to get from Zakho. "She wandered penniless from door to door, begged bread to keep soul and body together, and died, at last, an unloved toothless, old hag." Then they add piously, "Greed is at the root of all evil, and covetousness bolts the gate to Paradise."

As for Zakho, everyone agrees *he* lived long, prospered, and the poor were his children. Then, one happy day, he wed a maiden as good as she was beautiful. In time, he had a quiverful of his own little ones.

To the end of his days Zakho was rich, but of all his possessions he loved best the little crimson silk purse that was his father's. "It brought me luck," he always told his children and grandchildren. Then he'd smooth the wee bright thing on his knee, trace the design with a forefinger, and tell the tale of the Raven, the Mountain of the Sun and all the jewels the small purse once held.

THE AFFABLE LION (Jordan)

St. Jerome did not encourage sloth. After he had journeyed from Rome to Bethlehem in the fifth century, founded a monastery in the village where Jesus was born, and gathered about him his own disciples he told them, "Prayer and praise — and busy hands — make good men better."

Mindful of their Abbot's words, the brothers praised God and labored diligently from dawn to dark. Each performed a task for the common good. Some plowed, planted seed, and harvested golden grain to make the barley meal and wheat flour for their daily bread. Others worked in the vineyards and made ruby wine for the Holy Cup, and for pilgrim and stranger as well. Still others, skilled as craftsmen, made goatskin sandals or spun and wove rough cloth and fashioned the brothers' coarse brown robes.

Yet busy as the brothers were, all living creatures within the holy wall were likewise busy. They, too, had their appointed tasks. The small giddy Donkey, who preferred play to work, hauled wood from the pasture each day. The ducks and hens laid eggs. The sheep gave wool, and the goats their milk.

And the bees gave honey. "God bless our dear bees," said the monks. For always on the great feast days of the church, Cook contrived tasty cakes of meal and honey.

"How better may we poor sinners celebrate the sweet life hereafter than with a taste of honey now?" the good cook asked on Easter. And come Epiphany, he added spices to the little cakes "in remembrance of the Magi's gift to Our Infant Jesus."

Brother Jocundus' task was to tend the Donkey. Each day he strapped panniers on her back and drove her down a steep winding path and into a pasture that lay above the caravan trail to Egypt. But though he settled in the shade with a prayer book, he kept a sharp eye on his charge. If curiosity took her to the ledge at the far end of the field and she peered down at passing camels and men, he speedily fetched her back. "If you don't take care, you'll fall and break a leg," he chided, rubbing her long velvet ears. "Worse yet, a wicked driver will see your pretty face, climb the rocks and steal you!" Then he told her to play and stuff her stomach while she could. "Beasts, like brothers, must work," he said. "You'll carry a burden when we go home."

And so the ass did. As she plodded uphill before vespers, only her tiny feet were visible beneath the bristling load of fagots and sticks. Her step was slow and spirit unwilling. Then Brother Jocundus spoke kindly. "You serve God well today, little one. Your wood will kindle the fire, Cook will bake bread, and the poor of Bethlehem feast well tomorrow."

As if the small beast understood, she flopped her ears forward, quickened her pace, and entered the courtyard almost at a trot. Then followed the best part of her day. While the monks patted and praised her, Brother Jocundus removed her load. Then he bedded her down in her stall with fresh grain, fresh water and an affectionate pat.

One evening before sunset, St. Jerome paced, as usual, in the garden with the brothers, meditating, reading from the Scriptures, and expounding on holy truths. Suddenly the fearsome roar of a wild beast somewhere outside the cloister shattered the peace within. "Fear not, my sons, God will protect us," the Abbot said when the monks blanched, crossed themselves, and looked around in confusion.

But as the roars drew closer, the anxiety of the monks increased, and Brother Jocundus wailed, "It's a lion, come from the wilderness to devour us! And I forgot to lock the gate!"

Now, as if to realize the brothers' worst fears, the gate pushed open slowly. A huge Lion with tawny fur and amber eyes entered the courtyard, limped toward the huddled monks, and roared.

The monks were too terrified to see the great beast's limp or hear the anguish in his roar. Only the Saint saw and heard, and stood quietly as the Lion advanced. The brothers gathered up their brown skirts and flocked like frightened sparrows through the cloister door. Then they bolted it securely.

And now St. Jerome, alone in the garden with the Lion, touched the cross on his breast. Then, as an abbot greeting a pilgrim at the gate, he stepped forward and said, "You come to us in need and shall receive our help." The next instant — when the beast whimpered and gazed at him with pleading eyes — he saw that one great forepaw dangled limply, for it was pierced through by a thorn and woefully swollen.

"Ah, my poor friend, this will take courage," cried the Saint, and knelt to examine the festering paw. At last he extracted the thorn. And though the pain was very great, the beast seemed to understand the holy man was trying to help him. Gradually his roars subsided; he uttered low moans and licked his rescuer's hand. "And now you need care," St. Jerome said, stroking the tawny mane. "You shall stay with us till the wound heals. When you can defend yourself, you shall return to the wilderness."

Thereupon, he led the beast to the cloister door and commanded the monks to open it. "Our guest suffers, the paw festers and there is no time to lose," the Abbot said. Fearfully the brothers opened the door, mumbled excuses, and hung their heads in shame. But the Saint waved them aside. "Hurry, fetch water, bathe the wound, and bind it with salve," he said. "Then feed our visitor, prepare a bed of straw in the pilgrim cell, and see that he rests well."

"That was how the Lion came to live with St. Jerome and the holy men of Bethlehem," say the old storytellers to this day. Then they go on to tell how, thanks to the brothers' tender care, the wounded paw healed. But when the Saint declared the beast well and tried to return him to the wilderness, he refused to go.

As though born to cloister life, the Lion came and went freely and was docile and obedient. As a domestic creature, he mingled with the fowl and sheep, and from the first, he showed special affection for the little ass. As for food, though on certain days St. Jerome allowed the Lion meat, the beast learned to like roots and grains and even bread.

"The Affable Lion," the monks fondly called their new brother. For soon he padded the corridor on velvet paws during Vespers. When he followed the Abbot, his step was majestic, his head high. And at night when the Saint labored late, the beast sat at his side, licked his hand when he wearied, and led him at last to bed, clutching the Saint's robe in teeth.

There never was such a beast — or one more beloved. But as time passed, a problem faced St. Jerome. "What useful task can a lion perform for the good of our community?" he asked the brothers one day.

In the silence that followed their Abbot's words, each monk pondered the question. Brother Jocundus was the first to have an idea — so splendid his moon face was wreathed in smiles. "The Donkey needs tending, the Lion's clever, and they love each other," he said. "I can soon train him to take her to graze, pick up fagots, and fetch her home with brimming baskets. That way the Lion can replace me as shepherd, and I can work in the fields with the other brothers," he concluded.

Pleased with the proposal, the Abbot nodded. "Well said, Brother Jocundus. We are shorthanded. I am convinced now more than ever that God, whose ways are mysterious, sent the Lion to help us, rather than for healing of his paw."

To this the monks agreed — all save Brother Paul. *He* seldom believed good of anyone. "A lion's a lion," the old man muttered dourly. "You can teach tricks, turn growls to purrs, and *think* you've changed a wild beast's nature, but — "

"For shame, Brother Paul!" St. Jerome rebuked him.

From the start, the Lion proved a born shepherd. Each morning he trotted his charge from the courtyard, down the winding path and into the pasture. He stretched in the shade with eyes wide and ears alert and allowed her time to nibble and play awhile. Jackals and wolves shunned the field. When he roared, thieves scuttled, and if the little ass turned toward the ledge, a sharp growl brought her back.

Before Vespers each evening, the Lion drove the little Donkey home, her panniers loaded to the eartips with branches and sticks. Then the brothers ruffled his mane, whispered words of praise, and Cook tossed juicy tidbits into his jaws. "There never was a more affable beast," he chuckled.

"Or a trustier shepherd," Brother Jocundus declared proudly. "He looks after the ass better than I!"

As the weeks and months passed, the Lion continued to perform his task faithfully, took pride in his work, and the brothers loved and trusted him. Then, one awful day, everything changed.

That day, as always, the Lion drove the Donkey to pasture. But once he'd stretched out in the shade to watch her nibble and roll, excessive drowsiness overcame him. He had stayed up later than usual with the Saint, the previous night. And to make matters worse, the air was heavy, the sun hot, and the bees buzzed monotonously in a nearby patch of clover.

Trying to keep awake, the Lion snapped at a fly, switched his tail, and shifted position. But all in vain. The harder he tried to prop his eyes open, the more they drooped. When a caravan approached with tinkling bells, raucous shouts and yells, he was drowsing. He was sleeping soundly moments later, when a camel driver climbed into the pasture, glanced around furtively and, not noticing the Lion, grasped the Donkey's bridle and made off with her.

How long the beast slept he didn't know. But he awoke with a start and a sense of disaster. And when he didn't see his charge anywhere — after he'd searched the pasture, the road below and the woods — he ran up and down uttering frantic roars and doleful howls.

It was late when the Lion gave up his search and dejectedly plodded back to the abbey, tail between his legs and head bent in shame. Vespers had passed when he turned the last bend in the road, and the monks — pacing anxiously before the gates — surged forward. "Ah, here comes our Lion — without his charge," Brother Paul cackled mirthlessly.

"Where is our little Donkey?" shouted Cook. "What has happened to her?"

"As if you need ask!" Brother Paul sneered. "A lion's a lion, as I've said before. From the guilty look on yon beast's face, it's easy to guess where our Donkey is!"

"Then don't come home expecting *me* to feed you!" roared Cook in fury and tried to drive the Lion away. "Get back to the wilderness, savage brute that you are, and don't ever darken this holy house again."

Brother Jocundus wailed, "Alas, our trusty shepherd has devoured the Donkey!"

"SILENCE!" thundered St. Jerome, who just then stepped from the shadows. "For shame — to accuse a dumb animal unable to speak for himself of so hideous a crime! Until you find evidence of his guilt, say no more," he concluded, embracing the dejected Lion. "And may God judge you more mercifully than you judge this poor beast!"

"But — where is our Donkey?" clamored the brothers.

"That, God shall reveal to us in His good time," the Saint replied. "Do not nag the Lion," he entreated. "Treat him with kindness and do not add to his obvious misery. Until we learn why he failed to bring the Donkey home, his penance shall be to sleep in her stall and perform her task." Thereupon he instructed the brothers to make a harness with baskets attached, so the Lion could gather wood in her stead.

"Aha, our King of the Beasts will learn what it's like to be a beast of burden," said Cook later, and fed the Lion grudgingly.

In the weeks that followed, the monks treated the Lion as a common beast. Even after they'd combed the countryside for evidence of his crime and found nothing — no blood spots, shreds of hide or even gnawed bones — they looked upon him with suspicion.

Each morning the Lion slouched through the gate, the basket flippity-flopping at his heels. Each evening he hauled a heavy load up the hill. And now the brothers didn't praise him, toss tidbits into his jaws, or allow him to pace the corridors. "Ahh-h, our Lion is repenting for his sins!" they said, pausing at night in their prayers to listen to the howls of loneliness and despair from the Donkey's stall.

During those dreadful days only the Saint understood the Lion's humiliation, believed him innocent, and tried to comfort him. "Courage, dear friend," said he, ruffling the tawny mane. "God's ways are mysterious — but always just."

The Lion was to learn the truth of the holy man's words weeks later. The beast had just completed his usual futile search of pasture and woods, slumped to the ground, and was brooding about his comrade's mysterious disappearance, when faraway sounds brought him to his feet with a growl. Rumbling with excitement, he tore off the hated harness, leaped to the ledge, and crouched above the road. Before he slept soundly the day the Donkey disappeared, he vaguely remembered bells, shouts and the hoarse yells of men!

The Lion waited, muscles taut, spine tingling and eyes fixed on the bend of the road. The sounds grew closer, more distinct. Soon a string of seven camels, with a small donkey harnessed before them and men running alongside, rounded the bend. And when the Lion recognized the Donkey as his lost companion, his growls turned to roars of rage, and he thrashed the ground with his tufted tail.

The caravan advanced slowly, the plodding ass stumbled, and the fellow beside her brandished a stick and yelled. It was then that the Lion leaped to the road with blood-curdling roars.

Tumult and confusion followed. The men shrieked, the camels snorted, and the little Donkey, overjoyed to see her friend, brayed lustily. As for the Lion, *he* continued to roar, bounded up and down the road with bared teeth and glaring eyes, and chased the terrified traders into hiding. At last when he had cleared the way — with harm to neither man nor beast — he took charge of the caravan.

And now the quaking merchants, peering from behind boulders and through the branches of trees, saw the fierce beast turn into an amiable

shepherd. With friendly growls, gentle nudgings and the poke of a velvet paw, he soothed the trembling camels. When he'd straightened the sagging line, he took his place behind the beasts. With a triumphant roar to the little Donkey in the lead, he drove them away.

The owners of the caravan gnashed their teeth and looked on in helpless rage. Not until they saw the Lion turn the animals off the road and into the steep winding path up the hill did they creep from hiding. "By the Prophet's beard," declared the first man able to find voice. "The Donkey belongs to the Christian fathers yonder!"

"And so does the Lion, who all but tore us limb from limb," a second said shakily.

"Now all is lost — camels, the oil bought in Egypt and the money spent!" wailed a third, beating his breast.

"Unless we pay a visit to the abbot, invent a tale, and claim our beasts and goods," the owner of the caravan said with a crafty smile.

In the monastery, meanwhile, the brothers paced the cloister with their Abbot and pondered holy truths. All at once, loud joyous brays outside the walls, the Lion's deep exultant roar and jingling bells interrupted their meditations. "God has wrought a great miracle," said St. Jerome, his face shining, and the good men flew to the gate.

And, "God be praised," the monks shrilled the next moment. "Our Lion has brought back our Donkey, alive and well!" And so he had — for there she stood, before their eyes, harnessed to seven gangling camels. And there, leaping at their heels, was their trusty shepherd, the Affable Lion!

Before the brothers recovered from the wonder of the miracle, the little Donkey tossed her head, flipped her ears, and demurely led the camels into the courtyard. They sank to their knees. And now the Lion leaped toward the Saint. "Behold, he has proved his innocence," said the Abbot, and the monks, filled with remorse and shame, hung their heads before the beast they had wronged.

But the Lion, pleased at the way things had gone, showed ill will to none. He bounded from brother to brother and accepted their apologies with the graciousness that befitted the King of Beasts. "Forgive my meanness," choked Cook, to whom the Lion went first.

Last of all, the Lion went to Brother Paul. And when the old man embraced him, buried his face in the yellow mane, and sobbed, "F-forgive me. And may God forgive my sins and help me judge myself before I judge others," the beast licked the tears from the withered cheeks.

When the Lion had finished his rounds, St. Jerome gave instructions. "Minister to our guests," he said. "Remove their packs and give them water and food. They have journeyed far and are weary. And soon we shall receive other guests, their masters," he added and bade Cook spare no pains in preparing food and drink. "They, also, will be weary and need entertainment."

"That night the joy at the monastery was exceedingly great," say the storytellers of Bethlehem. Well before the moon hung like a silver ball in the sky and flooded the cloister with eerie light, the monks had tended the camels, put their beasts to bed, and were bustling from kitchen to cellar and back again.

The Lion had feasted sumptuously and curled himself three times round on sweet herbs in the pilgrim cell. And now his happy snores sounded like giant purrs. As for the little Donkey, *she* was in her stall. With full stomach and crib bursting with barley, she dreamed of the morrow — munching grass, playing, and kicking her heels.

In the kitchen Cook stirred the contents of a huge pot, the monks polished goblets on their sleeves and sniffed the fragrance of baking bread and basting lamb. A knock at the gate wreathed their faces in smiles and sent Brother Jocundus scurrying to open it.

The shamefaced traders, huddled in the moonlight, eyed the brother uneasily. The owner of the caravan twisted the fringe of his sash and said, "We would see your abbot. The hour is late, but our business urgent."

"He is expecting you," said Brother Jocundus and led them into the Saint's presence.

After the men had prostrated themselves at the Abbot's feet, he greeted them kindly and assured them their goods and camels were safe. They appeared even more uneasy. And when he pressed them to tarry and partake of refreshments before they went their way, their leader, bent on putting the matter in the best possible light, lied glibly. "May Allah bless you, kind Father, but 'tis more to ask forgiveness for taking your Donkey by mistake than to claim our property, that we come at this late hour. On our way to Egypt we found the beast — which we discovered was yours — lost and alone on the road. Out of pity we took her with us, lest wolves devour her and —"

"Because you wanted a donkey," the Abbot said severely and discoursed at length on such virtues as honesty and truth. "But now you shall break bread with us," he concluded.

But the leader of the traders, ashamed of their greed, beat his breast and cried, "May Allah have mercy on us and help us make amends for our evil deed. Before we accept your hospitality, kind Father, we beg *you* to accept a gift in token of our faith. We wish to share our oil from Egypt — three-and-twenty full measures — so you will have enough oil to keep your lamps full until we pass this way, twelve months hence."

When St. Jerome thanked the merchants for their generosity, their leader added, "Not only next year, but also for years to come, shall we remember this promise."

And so the camel drivers did, according to the old legend. They broke bread with the Abbot and his monks, he blessed them, and they departed in peace with their beasts and goods. And for many years thereafter, oil from Egypt burned brightly in the lamps of the holy house at Bethlehem.

And now that the Lion had brought their Donkey back, the brothers searched their hearts and grew in grace. Each man, at last, saw so clearly the beam in his own eye that he no longer sought the moat in another's. The prayer "Forgive us our debts as we forgive our debtors" took on a new meaning for the monks.

The Affable Lion again held his head high, trod the corridors with majestic step, and followed the Saint everywhere. As for the beast's charge, the small willful Donkey, *she* was a changed creature! After the fright of her capture, she obeyed her shepherd and never strayed or grumbled about her task.

When at last St. Jerome finished his great work on earth, God called him home. And then, lest he be lonely without his faithful friend, He called the Affable Lion to keep him company.

About the Author

DOROTHY GLADYS SPICER is a folklorist, who is well known for her stories and her work in peasant crafts and folk background. She majored in art history and languages at Vassar, studied archaeology at Radcliffe and folk arts and native festivals in many towns and villages of Europe and the Orient. There she carried on special research under folklore experts of the various countries.

Dorothy Gladys Spicer is the author of many books and articles on folk festivals, customs and foods. Her books include: 46 DAYS OF CHRISTMAS, 13 WITCHES, 13 MONSTERS, 13 GIANTS, 13 GHOSTS, 13 GOBLINS, 13 DEVILS, 13 JOLLY SAINTS, and THE OWL'S NEST: Folktales from Friesland.

About the Artist

BARBARA MORROW grew up in Cleveland, Ohio, and studied art at the Cleveland Institute of Art. With her husband and two sons, she has lived for twenty years in Kent, Ohio, where her husband teaches at Kent State University. THE KNEELING TREE is the third children's book Mrs. Morrow has illustrated.

Of her technique Mrs. Morrow says: "I literally find the parts of my picture by staring hard at rubbings of a piece of wood and play around with them in the manner of a collage until I arrive at the final forms and arrangement."

Also by DOROTHY GLADYS SPICER

THE OWL'S NEST
Folktales from Friesland
Illustrated by Alice Wadowski-Bak

"Friesland, the northernmost province of the Netherlands, provides the seven entertaining tales expertly told by the author. The practicality and common sense of the Dutch people and their folklore deities are reflected in the no-nonsense quality of the magic described in the tales. . . . All of the stories make good reading . . . attractive black and white illustrations enliven the texts."

— *Library Journal*
(Recommended star)

Best Books of Spring 1969   *Library Journal*